MW01254545

THE
DEEP
WOODS

THE
DEEP·
WOODS

Tim Pratt

2015

Published in April 2015 by PS Publishing Ltd. by
arrangement with the author. All rights reserved by the author.

FIRST EDITION

ISBN
978-1-84863-870-9 (Signed Edition)
978-1-84863-869-3

Design and layout by Alligator Tree Graphics.
Printed and bound in Great Britain by TJ International Ltd. Padstow

PS Publishing Ltd / Grosvenor House / 1 New Road /
Hornsea, HU18 1PG / England

editor@pspublishing.co.uk • www.pspublishing.co.uk

THE
DEEP
WOODS

For my son.

1

RYAN GOT SEPARATED FROM THE REST OF HIS PARTY when the queen of the swamp hags cast her traveling mist-spell, transporting everyone to random parts of the Endless Forest. He crept to the top of a ridge in the moonlit woods, hoping to spot some familiar landmark from the higher elevation, because this whole area was blank on his map.

He didn't see anything he recognized—but at the base of the hill, standing by a stream, stood the legendary Silver Stag, one of the rarest spawns in the woods. If the rest of his party were here, they would have argued about who got to kill the stag and take its loot, but since he was alone, there was no contest. The guys were going to be *so* jealous.

The Silver Stag—bigger than Ryan himself, with an enormous rack of silvery antlers that sparkled like frozen moonlight—was tough, but Ryan thought his gear was up to the job. He'd have to use the last of his enchanted elf-shot arrows, but what else was he saving them for? There was a 50 percent chance the stag would drop the epic headpiece called "Herne's Second-Best Helm," which would allow Ryan to summon his own miniature Wild Hunt once a day, a horde of half-sized monsters that both looked awesome and could help him beat some of the world's toughest enemies. There was also a tiny chance the Silver Stag would surrender before Ryan actually killed it, offering itself as a ridable mount, which would give Ryan the ability to travel through the Endless Forest at the speed of moonlight—which worked out to about 500 percent faster than running speed.

His hands trembled a little on the keys as he took aim with his bow.

"Rye!" his dad shouted from the bedroom doorway. "It's a beautiful day, kid, and we won't have many more of those this year. Why don't you go outside?"

"In a minute, Dad," Ryan said, half-whispering, as if raising his voice might startle the Silver Stag on his screen away.

His dad came up behind him and whistled. "Whoa, son, that's the Silver Stag! Kill it!"

Ryan clicked his mouse and pressed one of his hotkeys and unleashed a barrage of enchanted elf-shot on the screen. Tiny darts flew at the stag, but it shimmered and transformed into a shaft of moonlight before any of the arrows struck home. Ryan howled in frustration as his dad patted his shoulder. "Should've attacked from concealment," his dad said. "You could've used the surprise bonus. Mystical deer have a crazy-high dodge rating."

"I used the last of my good arrows on that," Ryan said. "I totally wasted them!"

"I never thought it was fair, the way your arrows just disappear," his dad said. "I mean, in real life, you can pick up your arrows after you shoot." He scratched his chin. "Then again, in real life, there aren't magical arrows with tiny mouths that bite whatever you shoot at—or magical deer, or the Wild Hunt, or swamp hags, or moon goddesses, or anything. So it's kind of a trade-off. Anyway, you're done with the Endless Forest today. Go out and look at the real forest for a while."

Ryan spun around in his chair and scowled. "I heard you tell Mom you were going to play *WHO* all day today." Ryan had only been allowed to play *WHO*—*Wild Hunt Online*, a massively multiplayer online fantasy role-playing game mostly set in and around and underneath a dark and magical forest—for a few months, but his mom and dad had been playing for years. They said they only played to keep in touch with their old college friends on the other side of the country, but Ryan knew they loved the game as much as he did. His dad played more often, but his mom was better—her guild was one of the top-ranked on the server.

"True," his dad said. "My guild's descending into the Cauldron of Death to fight the Triple Witch. We've been planning it for weeks. But, see, I'm all grown up. My mind's *already* been rotted by a lifetime of video games and TV. There's still hope for you, which is why we only let you play an hour a day. Go outside, run around, climb a tree—but not too high, you know your mom—make a bow and arrow out of reeds and fishing line or something. Use your imagination, so you can grow up to make games like this instead of just sitting around playing them."

Sighing, Ryan turned back to his keyboard and tapped out a quick farewell to the friends in his group. He didn't mention how he'd almost gotten the Silver Stag. They'd just give him crap about failing to kill it.

He slid off his chair and picked up his gray hoodie from the bed. It was a Saturday in late October, not too cold, but the air had a little bit of a bite. He slouched through the house, past his mom, who was arranging and rearranging way too many decorative gourds and miniature pumpkins on the dining room table, and into the kitchen, where he grabbed a bag of trail mix from the cupboard and filled up a water bottle. "Dad's making me go *outside*," Ryan said, trying to make it clear he'd rather be doing anything else, even going to the dentist or visiting smelly Great-Aunt Rhoda.

"Good," his mom said cheerfully, putting one gourd on top of a pile of other larger gourds. "It's a beautiful day. Come back before dark."

It wasn't quite ten in the morning. "Dark is, like, eight hours away," he pointed out.

"Oh, of course. I'll call you when lunch is ready then, and you can come in long enough to eat."

"Way to make me feel welcome, Mom." Ryan stepped over their black Labrador retriever, Gertie, sleeping in front of the side door as usual. They'd gotten Gertie when Ryan was a baby, and they'd grown up together, playing in the yard for years, but now Gert was almost eleven and very much an old lady, with lots of white hair in her muzzle, and as far as they could tell she'd gone entirely deaf a few months back. He gave her a scratch behind the ears before stepping out into the autumn morning.

They lived a few miles outside town on a couple of acres of land, backed up against a sprawling patch of forest his dad said belonged to nobody in particular, as far as he knew. Ryan liked the woods, and when his cousin Chris had visited over the summer, they'd spent whole long days out there—they'd been warriors, and soldiers, and jungle explorers, and monster-hunters, and shipwreck survivors on a desert island. It wasn't *quite* as much fun in the woods alone, certainly not as fun as playing *Wild Hunt Online*, but it was better than hanging around the backyard climbing on the rusted swing set. He hurried past the spider-filled woodpile, past the sagging clothesline, and on into the woods.

The Endless Forest in the game was eternally green, except for the places it was locked in winter, but in the real forest, only the pine trees were green now. All the dogwoods and maples and oaks were turning shades of red and orange and gold—fall colors, Halloween colors, fire colors. Brown curls of dried leaves crunched under the soles of his sneakers, and from somewhere far off he could smell woodsmoke, though it hardly seemed cold enough to need a fire.

In another month it would be, though. Soon the branches would be bare, and then there would be ice storms, wrapping the branches in transparent frozen shells, just like the ice armor you could get from defeating Jack Frost in the game. Eastern North Carolina almost never got snow, but it got ice, and sleet, and freezing rain, and yeah, this probably was one of the last nice sunny days they'd have for a while. But he'd still rather be playing with his friends inside than playing alone outside.

He crunched through the dead leaves along one of his usual trails, clear of poison ivy and only obstructed here and there by vines of briars. He knew the woods were full of squirrels, a few deer (dull brown, not silver), some snakes, wild pigs who'd escaped from local hog farms, and lots of birds, but today it seemed like he was the only living thing under the branches. After a while the trees got denser, and when he looked back, he couldn't see his yard anymore. He was probably less than half a mile from his own back door, but it felt like a lot more.

Without thinking about it, he wandered to the gnarled tree that held the old deer stand. The stand was an ancient wooden platform with low walls on three sides. A few wooden boards hammered into the tree trunk revealed where a ladder *used* to be, back when hunters had used this as a place to wait and watch for deer, but the rungs were so old and rickety that Ryan mostly just clambered up the branches. He had a little plastic tarp up there to keep the rain off, and a box of granola bars, some comics, a water gun, and a slingshot. He and Chris had used the stand as a pirate ship, jungle fortress, moon base, and knight's castle, but it was mostly just the clubhouse.

He climbed the ladder and found a boy about his age, skin white as paper and black hair, eating one of the granola bars and reading his comics. The boy wore what Ryan thought of immediately as old-timey clothes, like something out of a movie about the Amish or people from the past.

Ryan knew all the kids around here, and this wasn't one of them. There weren't that many—Ryan's family had neighbors, but they couldn't see anybody else's house from their own front yard, not this far out of town—and none of the other kids were within four years of Ryan's age.

"Uh," Ryan said. "Hey. What are you doing in my clubhouse?"

The boy looked up, not frowning or smiling or scowling or anything. "Clubhouse? You are in a club?"

"Well, no. I mean, I just call it the clubhouse."

"So it is more of a *boy* house," the boy said. "In which case, I am just as qualified to be here as you."

The woods didn't belong to Ryan, and neither did the deer stand, so even though he felt like his private space had been invaded, he just shrugged. "Those are my comics you're reading though."

"Penny dreadfuls in full color," the boy said, as if talking to himself. "And this strange bread is yours too?"

"Granola bars? Yeah."

"I apologize for taking your things," he said. "I always pay my debts. Here, I ask that you take this in exchange." The boy put a big dirty coin down on the plank floor of the clubhouse.

Ryan finished climbing up and took the coin in his hand. It was heavy, with a tree branch on one side and a face made of leaves and branches on the other. "Is this some kind of old money?"

"Not that old, where I am from," the boy said.

"It's cool," Ryan decided, and put the coin in his jacket pocket. "Thanks. You can have all the granola bars you want. I don't like them anyway." They'd belonged to Chris, really, though Ryan had sort of inherited them. "Did you just move here?"

"I have lived here for a very long time," the boy said.

9

"Huh." Ryan had heard that some homeschooled religious kids lived not far away, snake-handlers or something, so maybe he was one of those. That might explain why he was dressed in such old-fashioned clothes and why he talked so weird. "Well, nice to meet you. My name's Ryan."

"I am Silas."

"There's a kid named Silas in my class."

"All old things become new again in time." Silas took another bite of granola bar. Ryan settled back against one of the walls of the clubhouse, reached for a comic book he'd only read half a dozen times, and started flipping through it. Silas seemed like kind of a weird kid, but at least he didn't talk too much, and he *had* paid for the granola bars.

"Would you like to see something wondrous?" Silas said suddenly.

Ryan looked up, frowning. *Wondrous?* Who talked like that? "Like what?"

"Come with me." Silas went down the ladder without waiting for Ryan to answer. Ryan shrugged, put his comic away, and climbed down after him. Silas was already setting off into the woods, not on one of the old deer paths or hunting trails, but straight in among the trees, stepping over the roots and fallen branches and twists of briars.

Ryan followed him, trying to keep up—the weird kid was fast. Gradually the trees pressed in closer, growing thickly together, and the ground got steeper, making Ryan puff as he trudged uphill. He couldn't remember ever being in this part of the woods before, which was strange. The woods weren't *that* big—you could walk across them in forty-five minutes and come out in a farmer's field—and he would've sworn he'd seen every inch. Silas stopped at the top of the ridge, and Ryan paused a little down the slope, taking a long drink from his water bottle.

"There." Silas pointed, so Ryan trudged up beside him and looked where he pointed . . . and gasped at what he saw.

In the little valley on the other side of the ridge stood a tree bigger than anything he'd ever seen. There were supposed to be redwoods in California so large you could drive a car through tunnels hacked into their trunks, but you could sail a *battleship* through the center of this tree, if someone cut a channel. This was no redwood either, but an oak, so broad it looked like the wall of a castle. Ryan craned his head back, and the tree just went up, and up, and up, sprouting a thousand branches covered in autumn leaves. When a breeze blew, the leaves began to rain down, orange and gold and yellow, and Ryan heard a voice say, "Wow," and it took him a moment to realize it was his own.

"It is an astonishing sight," Silas said. "Even now, though I have seen it many times. Do you see the doors?"

"Doors?" Ryan said, but in that moment, he *did* see. There were black holes scattered along the trunk of the tree. He'd thought they were knotholes at first, but only because his mind couldn't comprehend the scale of the tree; the holes were all at least ten feet high.

"The tree is hollow, and yet still lives." Silas started down the slope toward the base of the tree. "I suppose it must be some magic of the Oakmen who once lived here, before the Horned Lord hunted them and drove them away."

"Oak...who? Horned what?" But Silas was already halfway down the hill, so Ryan followed him. This wasn't possible. He'd been all over these woods. He knew practically every inch. And a tree bigger than the city hall downtown? That wasn't something you could just... *not* notice.

"This is the largest of the Great Trees—at least the largest yet living." Silas rested his hand on the tree's bark. "I once walked all the way around it. Reckoning time can be difficult here, but I would say it took me the best part of a day to make that journey."

Ryan thumped the tree trunk with his knuckles. Solid as stone, and definitely real—not some trick or papier-mâché movie prop.

"Would you like to go inside?" Silas gestured toward a crack in the trunk, ten feet high and as wide as his outstretched arms. "No one lives there now. I sleep inside sometimes."

"You *sleep* there?"

"I am sorry," Silas said, lowering his head. "I should explain. I was once like you. I had parents, and a home. But then I was... " Silas chewed his lower lip, the first sign of nervousness—or really any emotion—he'd shown since Ryan met him. "I was taken. And even if I could go home, I no longer *have* a home. The world changed while I was gone. Every twenty or thirty years or so they let me step outside, for a day—like this day—just to see how much I have missed."

"What do you mean you were taken? You were, like . . . kidnapped? By some guys who live in a tree?" Ryan saw that kind of stuff on TV all the time, and read about it, but he'd never known anybody it had *happened* to.

"No, not by the Oakmen, and I was not kidnapped. I was . . . .enticed. Lured. The fairies here sang to me, in words written by a human poet, of course. They have no poetry of their own, only words stolen from others. They sang, 'Come away, oh human child, to the waters and the wild—'"

"With a fairy, hand in hand," Ryan sang, "For the world's more full of magic than you can understand." He grinned. "So you play *Wild Hunt Online*? That's the song from the opening cinematic."

"The Wild Hunt is nothing to play with. The ones who took me sang 'more full of weeping,' not 'more full of magic.'" Silas frowned. "You have heard this song as well? Were you stolen *too*?"

"Sure, sometimes." Ryan shrugged. "It happens. You're going about your business doing a quest or whatever, and you step into a ring of dandelions or walk over the wrong hill, the spooky music starts up, and bam, you're underground somewhere, trapped. But you just have to solve some puzzles, or play a mini game, or do a quest for one of the fairy bosses in order to get free again."

Silas grabbed him by the arm, his face all scrunched up and intense, and said, "You mean you were taken and you *escaped*?"

"Ow, hey, you're hurting me." Ryan pulled away. "Why are you freaking out? It's just a game."

"I love games," a voice boomed from the crack in the base of the vast tree. "Chasing games, and catching games, and eating games."

Ryan turned, eyes wide, and saw something pushing its way out of the crack. It looked like a person, but that couldn't be right, because it was bending over to step out, and if you had to bend over to walk through a door that was ten feet high, then that meant . . . That meant . . .

"Run!" Silas shouted, but Ryan was already scrambling up the hill back the way they came.

2

SOON—MUCH SOONER THAN SEEMED POSSIBLE, CON-
sidering how long it had taken to reach the ridge—they were over the
top and down the other side again, and the clubhouse was in sight. Ryan ran
toward it, thinking *I'll be safe there*, but really, the thing pushing its way
through the crack in the tree had been so tall it would be able to look into
the deer stand without even standing on tiptoe.

"Do not be afraid!" Silas called from a few steps behind him. "We are safe
now. Tom will not follow us here. It is forbidden."

Ryan slowed down and looked behind him, and he couldn't even see the
hill they'd climbed anymore again. "Tom? That thing's name is *Tom*?"

"Tom Dockin," Silas said. "His teeth are made of iron, and they say he eats
nothing but children, but . . . " Silas shrugged. "There *are* no children in the
forest, excepting myself and Gabriel, so I do not see how he could."

"Maybe there aren't any children because he *ate* them all." Ryan climbed
into the clubhouse and sat in a corner, hugging his knees to his chest and
staring at the toes of his sneakers.

Silas followed him and sat in the opposite corner. "I am sorry for that,
Ryan. I did not expect Tom Dockin to find us—he must have smelled me,
from the last time I slept in the Great Tree. There are greater dangers than
Tom in the Deep Woods . . . though even he is enough to end me."

"Tom," Ryan marveled again. "He should be named . . . monster-face.
Giant-man. Not *Tom*."

Silas nodded. "Perhaps he has other names. My mother told me he
was called Tom. She came from England, though her people were from

Ireland and Scotland, and she knew so many stories. When I was very young, I believed them all—in Tom Dockin and Rawhead-and-Bloody-Bones, who would come for me if I misbehaved. Nelly Longarms and Jenny Green-teeth, who waited in every stream and pond to snatch up boys who played where they shouldn't. The Boneless, also called the It, who would come for you if you traveled in dark or dangerous places alone. Herne the Horned Lord, and the Wild Hunt, and the elf-knights, and the salmon of wisdom . . . Mother told me all her old tales, but I stopped believing in them when I got older. I suppose it seems foolish to you, to believe in such things—in magic."

Ryan thought for a moment and said, "When I was really little I cut myself trying to walk through a mirror, like the girl from *Alice in Wonderland*. Kid stuff. At least, I thought it was kid stuff."

Silas nodded. "As did I. I stopped believing in such monsters, as I grew older . . . But some of them turned out to be very real. Tom Dockin among them."

Ryan looked up, into his new friend's eyes. "That place. With that tree. That wasn't these woods. We were in fairyland. Weren't we?"

"The place has many names," Silas said. "The Fields Beyond the Fields–though in this part, at least, there are few fields. The Deep Woods. Elfhame. The Perilous Realm."

"The Endless Forest," Ryan said. He began to grin. "Holy crap, Silas—it's the Endless Forest. Not exactly the same as the game, okay, but the place that inspired the game, like, for *real*."

"I do not understand. This game you mention—is it . . . a game of cards? A game of let's pretend?"

"More like let's pretend. Do you, ah . . . you know television?"

Silas shook his head.

Ryan chewed his lip. How did you explain a MMORPG to a kid who'd never even seen a *screen*? "You've seen puppet shows?"

"Of course."

"Great. It's like that—you sort of control a puppet. You can have a puppet who's a witch, or a hunter, or a warrior, or a wizard, or a magical healer—lots of different things. And you use the puppets to act out different stories and have fights with people controlling *other* puppets, and you solve puzzles, and take part in contests, stuff like that. And the, ah, puppet theater? The scenery or whatever? Is all stuff from fairyland, with swamp hags and monsters and elves and things."

"I think I see," Silas said. "You are familiar with the imaginary fairyland, which tells you something, perhaps, about the *real* fairyland."

"Yeah. I think. But I don't get it. We didn't step into a ring of mushrooms or go through a magical arch or, I don't know, climb through a mirror or crawl through the back of a magical closet or get picked up by a tornado and carried over the rainbow—so how'd we *get* here? To that other world?"

Silas frowned. "I do not think it is another world, exactly. It is just . . . the Deep Woods. Part of the woods you do not normally notice, that you cannot normally reach—just as I cannot normally reach *this* part of the wood, though I can see it from the other side, as if through a dirty window. I saw you playing here, so many times, and I always wished to join you in your games. I am . . . glad I met you today, Ryan. Perhaps we can just stay here, and play? As ordinary boys do? I would enjoy that."

Ryan stared at him. "Silas, you live in *fairyland*. That's awesome! Why would you want to play here? Why come back to the real world at *all*?"

Silas sighed. "I understand your feelings. At first, this world seemed wondrous to me as well. My old life was hard, Ryan. My parents were poor farmers. My elder sister died of fever. There were weevils in our flour, and fleas bit me in my bed. This place was so magical, at first. But it is sometimes a dark magic. The fairies are often cruel. Now I live in the woods, and eat mushrooms and berries and roots, or scraps scrounged from the tables of more powerful creatures. Some nights, the Wild Hunt runs baying through the woods, hounds racing through the trees, and I hide, because to the Hunt, everyone else is prey. Sometimes an elf lord finds me and forces me to work, serving in one of the great houses under the hills, or chopping wood, or polishing silver, or scrubbing pots. And . . . I miss my family. They have been gone for a long time. I will never see them again." Silas turned his face away, and from the way his breath hitched and snuffled, Ryan knew he must be crying.

Ryan went over beside Silas and patted him on the shoulder. "Hey, it's okay. We can . . . We can get you out of this. You don't like it in fairyland? So we'll figure out a way for you to escape."

Silas lifted his head. "You would help me?"

"As long as I get to see more of fairyland, yeah."

"I can take you anywhere," Silas said. "I have the freedom of the Deep Woods. But where would we begin?"

Ryan considered. "You just need to find someone wise to tell you how to accomplish whatever you're trying to do—a quest-giver. We need to look for a person who can tell you how to escape, and we'll probably have to trade something or do some dirty jobs for them, in exchange for the information we need. In the game, there's a place, they call it the goblin market, and it's supposed to be a great spot to get information. I've never been there myself—my character is too low-level, the goblins would just eat me—but I've seen my mom play there, and she says it's the starting point for all the major endgame quests. Is there any place like that in your version of fairyland?"

"There is the fairy market," Silas said. "It is frequented by all manner of bogies and trooping fairies, bartering objects from the ordinary to the magical, but humans are not usually welcome there. Gabriel and I have only ever reached it once—"

"Who's Gabriel? You mentioned that name before."

Silas nodded. "Gabriel Ratchet. The other boy in the Deep Woods. He has been there only half as long as I have . . . though still a very long time. He was stolen from his family too. We were friends, once. But Gabriel is . . . braver than me, and not very nice. He plays tricks and makes cruel jokes, and he has traded away many of his mortal memories to Black Annis, the hag of the hill caves, in exchange for fairy magic. Sometimes I talk to him anyway, because he is still more human than anyone else in the Deep Woods, but it is probably best if you do not meet him. He is very jealous of boys like you, who still live out in the wider world."

"Maybe we can help him get out too?"

Silas shivered. "I think the world is safer with Gabriel Ratchet locked away in the Deep Woods. He has freedom today too, only the second time the horned king, Herne, has ever granted him a liberty. Last time he ran as fast as he could and—what did he call it?—hitchhiked. He said he traveled miles and miles, and thought he would be free, but when the moon rose, he was transported back into the Deep Woods. It was after that failure to escape that he began visiting the blue-faced hag and learning magic. I do not know what he is doing today. Trying to find a way out of the woods, I suspect."

"Well, good luck to him. Let's go to this market of yours. If you've only got until the moon comes up to go back and forth between this world and that one, we'd better get moving." Ryan picked up his slingshot—he wanted some kind of weapon, and the water gun probably wouldn't be much good—and tucked it into his jacket pocket.

Silas clambered down out of the tree, and Ryan came after him. He wasn't entirely sure Silas's whole story was real. Ryan liked playing *WHO*, but he knew the difference between real life and virtual life. But his mom *had* told him the world of the game was based on old legends and stories and folklore, mostly from England and Ireland, and maybe some of those stories *had* been true? It didn't really make sense that creatures from the other side of the Atlantic Ocean would be living in the woods behind his house. But in the game, part of the story was that *all* forests were connected on some magical level, all part of the same vast wood that spanned worlds, and you could get to the Endless Forest through any stand of trees or patch of bushes anywhere, if you had the right charm or knew the right spell or had the right guide. It didn't seem *likely* . . . but Ryan had always wanted to believe in magic.

Still, he wasn't crazy. He knew Tom Dockin most likely wasn't a giant at all, but just some older boy messing with them. Silas was probably just a weird homeschooled kid playing a seriously hardcore game of let's pretend, but so what? Back when he was in college, Ryan's dad used to do something called LARPing, live-action role-playing, where he'd dress up like a wizard and run around the woods with his friends. The videos of his dad wearing a red robe and a pointy hat, throwing tennis balls while yelling, "Lightning bolt!" were incredibly lame—because it was his *dad*—but Ryan thought it sounded like fun. So if he and Silas were just acting out an escape from fairyland, that could still be pretty cool.

But that tree. The Great Tree. How could he explain that away?

This time Silas didn't lead him through the bushes, but along one of the many deer paths that wound through the woods. Ryan had been this way a million times, and knew it led to the place he called the Ballroom, a clearing with just a few stunted trees scattered around, their trunks all covered in a weird whitish-silvery fungus. A nice spot, and a natural home base for games of hide-and-seek or war. The clearing divided up the forest in a way too. On the western side, the woods were full of big trees for climbing, a meadow full of wildflowers, an awesome half-collapsed old shed, and a big creek with lots of rocks you could hop along and climb across. On the eastern side of the Ballroom, it was all thick briars and brambles, but if you managed to slash your way through, you could find places where the trees were so overgrown they blocked the light almost completely, and you could crawl around like you were in secret tunnels for what felt like miles.

The air was getting a little colder, that crisp bite that made the inside of your nostrils burn, and the smell of burning wood floated by on the breeze. Ryan and Silas walked on without speaking for a while. "There," Silas finally said, pointing. "You can see the stalls of the fairy market."

Ryan looked up from the trail and stared. The Ballroom was still there up ahead, but now, among the trees, there were tented booths like they had at the farmer's market, only these canopies were green and gold and blue and red and purple instead of boring white. "I don't get it," Ryan said. "This isn't the Deep Woods—I go here all the time."

Silas nodded. "I have seen you here. But you did not see me. The deep woods are not another world—just a part of this world you cannot usually see. And we probably will not be able to reach the stalls. Except for once, with Gabriel, I have never been able to do so. The tents and tables shrink when I approach, getting smaller and smaller as I get closer, instead of growing larger, as things normally do. By the time we get close enough to touch them, they will have disappeared completely. Getting to the market is like trying to hunt a rainbow, or to peel your own shadow off the ground."

But as they approached, the tents didn't disappear, and the voices of the sellers in their stalls grew louder. "Come buy, come buy!" they shouted, and called out the names of the fruit they had for sale, half of which Ryan had never heard of.

"This is . . . all different." Silas stopped before they entered the clearing. "The last time I made it here, there were elves and brownies and trooping fairies, shoemakers and goldsmiths and cooks baking meat pies in brick ovens, but nothing like this . . . like *them*."

"It's just like the market in the game." Ryan paused beside him. "I mean, *exactly*, only real. Those guys, the goblins—am I seeing this? Those aren't masks?"

Silas shook his head. "I do not think so."

The goblin men—who were mostly shouting "Come buy, come buy!" even though there weren't any customers in evidence—were all only partway human, with the bodies of men and monstrous heads and faces. One had the snout of a rat, and another the whiskered face of a black cat. There was a bear-faced goblin, and one with the starred nose of a mole, and—the creepiest-looking one—a goblin who had the head of a snail, complete with slimy, waving eyestalks.

"This is wild," Ryan said, but something about it bothered him. Somehow this didn't seem *right* . . . "Huh," he said. "It's kind of weird, Silas, but . . . I don't think these goblin guys should *be* in the real fairyland. When I watched my mom play this part in the game, she told me the goblin market is based on some poem by a woman named Christina something. Mom said most of the stuff in the game is from actual old legends, but some parts are taken from stories and plays and poems, with lots of bits stolen from Shakespeare and some guy named Yeats. Mom's always using the game to try and get me to read more, you know? I remember she gave me that 'Goblin Market' poem, and it was so *boring*, just lists of fruit and some junk about these girls who all had names starting with L, but the description of the goblin men was pretty cool. They were like *these* guys, all rat-faced and wombat-headed. But if this place comes from a poem, what's it doing in the *actual* fairyland?"

"Perhaps this Christina caught a glimpse of the Deep Woods," Silas said, "and wrote about what she saw. They say poets and artists can find this world more easily than others. But I confess, I have never seen these goblin men of yours before. The deep woods are full of glamours and illusions—perhaps it simply amuses the fair folk to appear in such forms today?"

"Maybe. We should be careful in there, though." They started walking again, along the path that wound between the tents and stalls. One goblin, with a wrinkled-apple face and the paws of a dog, held out a beautiful golden pear. "A morsel, ensorcelled?" he said, his voice croaking like a frog. "Best tasted, never wasted?"

"Uh, I don't have any money," Ryan said. "Do you know anybody around here looking for help from, you know, a couple of adventurers?"

"You have gold upon your head," the goblin said.

Across the path, another merchant with the face of a red parrot squawked angrily and began flapping his arms. "And so you shall soon be fed. Clip us a curl, and purchase the world."

"No need, no need!" shouted a dog-faced goblin, showing all his long teeth. "Taste my apples. The first bite's free!"

"Accept nothing they offer," Silas whispered. "Do not eat any food from this place. That is how they captured me forever, and Gabriel too—we tasted fairy food, and now we can never be free."

Ryan nodded. There were places in the game where there was free food, magical food that gave you special powers, but the food was really cursed, and there was a price to pay—some of the food gave you diseases if you didn't eat it every day, and some made you randomly teleport back to the place you'd first gotten the food, until you could find a witch or wizard to remove the curse. "No, thanks," he told the pear-seller and hurried along the booths with Silas, looking for . . . something. In the game, you could easily identify the non-player characters who gave you quests. They were surrounded by a sort of yellow aura, which turned into a blue aura after you talked to them and accepted a quest, and disappeared completely after you successfully completed the task they'd set for you: gathering the golden apples of the sun, capturing criminal pixies, stealing ingredients for a love potion, or whatever. (At higher levels, the quests were more like "Descend into the Cauldron of Death and Confront the Triple Witch" or "Gamble All Your Possessions Against Robin Goodfellow in a Game of Chance" or "Battle the Long Worm" or, at the very highest level, "Defeat Herne the Hunter and Retrieve His Antlered Helm.") But there was no telltale glow here. This *wasn't* a game, however much it might resemble one. Or, if it was a game, it was a game the fairy folk were playing with *him*.

The relative silence was what finally caught his attention. There was one booth that was actually more of a tent, draped in deep-red velvet, with a tiny opening through which firelight glinted. No goblin was shouting, "Come buy!" from in there, and Ryan paused and nudged Silas. "We should see who's inside." Without waiting for his new friend to respond, Ryan stood in the opening of the tent and said, "Hello? Can we come in?"

There was no answer, but the tent flap twitched open wider, and Ryan beckoned to Silas and ducked inside. The interior of the tent was close and warm, with a fire burning in a ring of stones in the middle of the floor, producing heat but no smoke. A man dressed in clothing made of tree leaves and green moss, with a long beard woven with twigs and berries, sat cross-legged on a pillow and gestured toward a pair of cushions near the door. Ryan and Silas sat, and Ryan squinted at the figure—who, while less inhuman than the goblins, didn't seem entirely like a normal man—until something clicked and he said, "You're Ghillie Dhu!"

"Gilly do?" Silas frowned. "I do not know that name."

"As you have spoken my name," the green-clad figure said, leaning forward closer to the firelight, "so shall I speak to you."

"It's okay," Ryan said to Silas. "He's one of the good ones. He helps people on quests—in the game, I mean. Usually he appears way back in the woods when you're totally lost, and he gives you a hint about what you should do next, but only if you greet him by name first. You have to pay attention to some of the dialogue way at the beginning of the game to find out his name too, and remember it when the time comes."

"I do not know this game of which you speak," Ghillie Dhu said. "But I sometimes give aid to lost travelers."

"We're not so much lost as we don't know where to start," Ryan said. "My friend Silas is trapped here. He was stolen by fairies, and he wants to know how to escape back to the, uh, wider world."

Ghillie Dhu stared at Ryan, then looked into the fire for a long moment. "What you ask is not easy. There are many trials to be faced between this meeting and any eventual success. Are you equal to the challenge?"

There was no button reading "accept quest" to click here, but Ryan knew enough to follow the form. "Yes. We accept the challenge."

"Then this is what you must do first," Ghillie Dhu began.

21

3

GHILLIE DHU PICKED UP A STICK FROM THE EDGE OF THE fire, blew gray ash off the end, and used the blackened end of the stick to draw on the ground in thick, clear lines. "You must go to the long barrow, where the fairy men and women are forever about their revels, and join them, but do not eat of their table or drink their wine. Find one of their cups and beg, borrow, buy, win, or steal it away." He sketched a picture of a cup on the ground, like one of Ryan's mom's wine glasses in profile. "The cup you need is of unusual color and unknown material, and you will know it because it resembles no other. Next, take this cup to the well of the moon, which is protected by Beag's three daughters." He sketched a crescent moon in the dirt, next to the cup. "You must fill the fairy cup with water from the well. To drink from the well is a great temptation and a great danger—the first taste gives you wisdom, and the second sip the gift of prophecy—but you are not to drink the water. Instead, you must carry the cup, without spilling a drop, to the hills beyond the swamp, where you will find the cave of the witch Gentle Annie." He drew a couple of curved lines that Ryan assumed were meant to be hills, though they looked just as much like seagulls or boobs. "Give Gentle Annie the cup of well water to drink, for she thirsts for it dearly, and once she is sated, she will show you the way to your freedom."

"Cup, water, witch," Ryan said. "You got all that, Silas? I should have brought something to write with."

"Farewell and good luck," Ghillie Dhu said, rubbing out the drawings in the dirt. "I hope I never see either of you again."

When they stepped out of Ghillie Dhu's tent, the rest of the goblin market was gone, with nothing left behind but smashed bits of fruit abuzz with hundreds of flies. Ryan was excited, bouncing on the balls of his feet, ready to get started on the quest.

But Silas was frowning and shaking his head. "I do not believe his words are true. This is just another trick of Herne's, to make me think I can escape. There is no leaving the fairy realm, Ryan. It is pleasant to pretend, to imagine, but—"

"What can it hurt?" Ryan said. "It *will* work, but even if it doesn't, at least you'll be doing something. It's better than being bored. And think of the amazing stuff we'll see!"

"Amazing, and awful, and terrifying," Silas said. "Barrows and witches and wells."

"I don't know. Gentle Annie doesn't sound like a bad person."

Silas laughed. "You cannot trust names here, my friend. Do you know what people call the fairies? The good folk, the gentry, the good neighbors, the honest folk, the men of peace—but they do not say such things because they are true. They say them to avoid giving offense, and to flatter the fairies."

"So you're saying Gentle Annie could be the kind of person who eats people and makes furniture out of their bones?"

"Yes," Silas said. "But no one dares call her Bone Chair Annie because they are afraid it might make her angry. I have never been to her cave, or into the caves of any of the hags and witches beyond the swamp. I cannot say if she is good, or bad—she is only a name to me, one I have heard once or twice in passing. But it is best to be cautious."

Ryan kicked a bit of melon and grinned. "You've survived here for . . . how long?"

"As those outside the Deep Woods reckon time? Perhaps a hundred years. Though it has sometimes felt like much more, and sometimes like much less."

"Right—you've made it that long. I doubt Bone Chair Annie will be the one to end your winning streak, especially now that I'm here helping you. I'm good at puzzles and trick questions. Besides, if we bring her a gift, she won't want to eat us. We'll get through this whole quest chain by lunchtime. Wait and see."

Silas began to smile. It was a shy sort of smile, like a kitten peeking out from behind a curtain, but it was there. "Your enthusiasm gives me confidence, Ryan. This can be a very slow and quiet place—when it is not a very loud and terrifying place—and it is easy to despair, but you give me hope."

Ryan slapped his back. "Good. So let's get started. Where's this long barrow? And what's a barrow, anyway?"

Silas blinked. "Ah. It is a grave mound, Ryan. A heap of earth piled atop a burial chamber."

"Oh." Ryan considered that for a moment. "That's so cool. Like a tomb?"

"Exactly like. But sometimes, if you venture into a barrow here, you find not a tomb, but a dwelling place for fairies."

The branches rustled on the eastern edge of the Ballroom, and Ryan looked over to see a giant, ten feet tall despite being hunched over, pushing his way through the trees. The giant was hideous, with a nose like a gnarled root and grinning teeth of dull-gray iron, dressed in a profusion of furry dead animal skins, but the giant wasn't the strangest thing—that was the red-haired, freckle-faced boy, perhaps a year older than Ryan and Silas, riding atop the giant's shoulders, holding onto the giant's enormous ears like reins. "Other times you just find a lot of dead people and rusty old weapons," the boy said.

The giant—Tom Dockin, Ryan assumed—growled and reached out toward them, but the boy riding him yanked the giant's ears, and Tom lowered his arms and grumbled. The boy said, "Who's your new friend, Silas? Aren't you going to introduce us?"

Silas stared wide-eyed at the giant. "This . . . This is Ryan. He lives outside the woods. The *ordinary* woods. And Ryan, this . . . . is Gabriel Ratchet. Gabriel, how have you tamed Tom Dockin?"

"Not tamed," Tom Dockin growled. "Making a *bargain*."

"That's right," Gabriel said. "We just made a little trade. Tom will serve as my mount and helper for a time, and in exchange, he gets to eat me."

"Delicious boy." Tom licked his lips—his tongue was covered in fungus like a rotten tree branch—and drool ran down over his chin. "When do I get to eat you?"

"When your term of service is done, Tom," Gabriel said patiently. "As we discussed, and as you swore." He leaned forward, propping his elbows on top of Tom's head. "So, Ryan, what brings you to the Woods beyond the Woods?"

"I'm going to help Silas escape," Ryan said. "We just met with Ghillie Dhu in there and . . . " He turned to point at the red tent, but it was gone, with just a burned-down fire circle in its place. "Oh. Well, he told us what to do." Ryan shrugged. "So we're going to do it."

"Sounds like you've really thought this through." Gabriel smirked, and he had this *tone*, like he knew something they didn't, or maybe like he was smarter than everyone else and laughing inside because they were too dumb to even realize it. "I can't wait to see how it works out for you."

Silas stared at the ground, digging in the dirt with his toe, and Ryan could tell that, in their relationship, Gabriel was the bully and Silas was the victim. It had probably been that way for a long time. Ryan didn't have much trouble with bullies anymore himself, but not because he had some secret to dealing with them—it was just that his worst bully, the meanest kid in school, had picked on a new girl last spring, pulling her hair, and she'd kicked him between the legs and made him fall down crying, and everyone had laughed at him. That had been the end of his bullying days, and a time of relative peace had descended on Ryan's school.

Kicking Gabriel in the crotch would be tricky, since that sensitive area was currently blocked by a kid-eating giant with iron teeth . Ryan said, "We've got to get going. See you around."

"I'm hurt, Silas. You're not going to invite me on your little adventure?"

Silas didn't look up. "I . . . Do you want to assist us, Gabriel?" He stole a glance at Ryan, who frowned. "With your fairy magic?"

"It's only fairy magic when fairies do it," Gabriel said. "When I do it, it's *Gabriel* magic. Thanks for the offer, Silas—it's nice to know some people are considerate—but I'm pursuing my own avenues of escape. I've got a very promising lead on something. I'll check in on you from time to time to see how you're doing." He yanked on Tom Dockin's ears. "Come, Tom. We have miles to go before you eat."

"My term of service," Tom Dockin said slowly, as he wheeled around and began stomping back toward the briar-filled part of the forest. "How long will it last?"

"As I said, it's an adjustable rate term," Gabriel replied. "With the exact period dependent on variables too numerous to mention. Now come along. There are some truly wicked thorns I need you to walk through."

After Tom and Gabriel were gone, Ryan said, "I don't like that guy. Why did you suck up to him?"

"I do not like him either," Silas said. "But I cannot risk his anger. He is not as powerful as the fairies, but he is far more powerful than I."

"Maybe Tom Dockin will eat *him*," Ryan said.

"It is possible. But Gabriel is luckier than most. Let us begin our journey before he returns." Silas set off north from the Ballroom, and Ryan didn't object, though he knew that path would lead them soon to a local farmer's back field, near a leaning old tobacco barn surrounded by thoroughly rust-encrusted bits of broken machinery. He wasn't entirely surprised when the familiar path gradually gave way to denser forest, with trees he'd never seen before—including some with long strips of peeling white bark. The breeze blowing through the branches made a sound like distant whispering. There were times when the trees were so close that Ryan and Silas had to slip between the trunks sideways, and low-hanging branches seemed to pluck at Ryan's hoodie and hair as he passed. For all he knew, the trees really *were* tugging at him. He was comforted by the knowledge that trees didn't have teeth, or even mouths. Usually.

After a time, the trees thinned out and they reached another path, wider and with the remains of paving stones scattered here and there, as if it had once been a proper pathway before the forest dragged it back into being half-wild. They did reach a field soon, but it wasn't the overgrown and abandoned one Ryan was used to; the grass here was brown and dead, and long humps of earth were scattered around like artificial overgrown hills. "The barrow-lands," Silas murmured. "I don't come here often. Look at the sky."

Ryan shaded his eyes and peered upward. The sky was cloudless, but it was a blue so pale it was practically gray, and the sun seemed somehow diminished, almost watery, as if seen through the distorting glass of a shower door. "This place is freaky," he said, and somewhere a crow cawed harshly, though Ryan couldn't tell if it sounded more like it was agreeing with him or making fun of him. "So, uh, how do we get in? Do we need shovels or something?" If they had to dig into one of those humped hills, it was going to take a while, especially with no tools.

"There's usually a door," Silas said. "We want the long barrow." He led Ryan toward a low mound that extended as far as Ryan could see toward the horizon. The barrow was about as tall as his dad's pickup truck, and if there were any revelries going on inside, the fairies had great insulation—there was no sound but the mournful wheeze of wind in the dead grass and the occasional crow call. They walked along the mound until Ryan finally spotted a little door set in the side of the barrow. He'd been expecting a round door, for some reason, like in a hobbit hole, but this was a square door made of heavy wood with moss growing in the cracks between the planks. There *was* noise behind the door, the sound of music and laughing voices.

"Last time I went into one of these mounds, I was dressed in a bright green coat and forced to serve drinks to the guests," Silas said.

"Posing as waiters. That's a great idea. We could steal a cup then, no problem." Ryan pushed the door open and stepped inside.

He'd expected gloom and maybe some cool bones, with or without carved stone coffins, but inside the hill there was a brightly lit house, complete with hanging chandeliers filled with candles and long tables groaning with food and dozens of people—except they weren't quite people—spinning by dancing. They were dressed like the actors in the costume dramas his mom liked, long poofy dresses and lots of jewels for the women, weird pants and suit coats and ruffly shirts for the men. The floor was polished stone, the ceiling was *way* too high to fit inside the mound, and there were huge floor-to-ceiling windows . . . though they just looked out on the rocky dirt walls of the inside of a hill. The only light came from the candles, and from a few of the dancers themselves, who glowed like they had flashlights switched on under their skin. Some of the dancers had pointy ears, and a few had tails, and others had hooves like goats (which somehow didn't seem to hurt their dancing at all). Two or three looked like trees stuffed into suits, with curling branches and leaves poking out of the collars and sleeves and leg holes, though they moved as easily as the others did. On a raised platform near one of the vast windows, musical instruments were playing themselves, violins bobbing in the air and cello bows sawing back and forth without need of hands. The dancers moved through the steps together in groups as if they'd practiced them a thousand times, and their motion reminded Ryan of the way a flock of birds in the sky could change direction together all at once.

Waiters—including a couple of old, exhausted-looking humans dressed in rags—moved among the fairies on the edges of the dance floor, the ones who weren't dancing, offering drinks. Their trays all held long narrow glasses, though, none of them cups, and certainly none unlike all the other cups, of which there were none. "Maybe we should check the kitchen?" Ryan said, pushing the door shut behind them.

"There is no kitchen," Silas said.

"Then where do all the food and drink . . . Right. Fairyland." It made sense. In the game, Ryan could conjure food and drink by magic, and he didn't even play one of the fey races, just a human hunter who'd strayed into fairyland by mistake—being a human gave you certain advantages, like being able to use iron weapons, and disadvantages, like not having natural fairy magic. But humans in the game could learn some fairy magic . . . not unlike the way Gabriel Ratchet had here. *That* was a crappy thought. "Then I guess finding a cabinet full of cups isn't going to happen. We'd better keep looking around."

"What if there is no special cup?" Silas said. "What if Ghillie Dhu was only mocking us, as I feared?"

"Then we'll knock his tent down and throw rotten goblin fruit at his head. Come on, let's look." They skirted along one wall of the house, weaving among the legs of the revelers, who paid them little attention, except for aiming the occasional half-hearted kick at them to move them out of the way. Ryan kept his eyes open, but didn't see any cups, let alone any of unusual color or material.

But when they neared the end of the long house, he saw a creature sitting in a chair in the corner. Not quite as big as Tom Dockin but larger than the revelers, the figure had a crooked tin crown on his head, warty gray skin like an elephant, ears like the wings of a bat, enormous watery sad-looking eyes, a nose like a dead banana slug, and a downturned, lipless mouth. His ears rose and fell as he sighed, his many-fingered hands resting on his bony, knobby knees. "I know him," Ryan whispered, elbowing Silas.

The creature reached over to a low table by his chair, picked up a cup—the color of a rainbow reflected in a mudpuddle, Ryan thought, or maybe just a strange shade of indigo—and took a sip before putting the cup back down.

"I have never seen such a creature before," Silas said. "Is it another of your goblin men?"

"No." Ryan grinned. He pulled Silas into the safety of the space underneath a long banquet table so they could talk without any fairies overhearing. "He's the Trow King. I've *done* this quest. In the game, it's called The Trow King's Treasure. Silas. We can *do* this."

4

"THIS IS SOMETHING YOU'VE DONE IN YOUR...PUPPET theater game?" Silas said doubtfully, crouching in the dimness under the table.

"Yeah, but I wasn't stealing a cup. I was stealing... I don't even remember. A treasure chest or something. But I remember *how* I did it. A lot of people try to fight the Trow King—"

"We cannot *fight*," Silas said, aghast. "He's bigger than the two of us combined!"

"Exactly. Trying to fight him is no good. In the game, if you attack him, he just beats you up—he's pretty much indestructible. But the object of the quest isn't to defeat him; it's to steal his treasure, and you don't *have* to fight. There are lots of quests like that, actually. My mom and dad say that's why *Wild Hunt Online* is a better game for kids than most of the other MMORPGs, which are all about fighting and killing. To beat the Trow King, you have to be clever. Some people go in with a partner, and one of them taunts the Trow King to distract him while the other grabs his treasure."

"We could do that, I suppose," Silas said. "Though risking the Trow King's ire is not a task I would volunteer for."

"It's okay—that trick doesn't work either. See, the Trow King has the ability to be in two places at once—he literally splits in two, so there are *two* Trow Kings. And even though each Trow King is only half the size of the original, they're actually *twice* as strong, so he—they—beats you up even faster. Same thing if there are three of you, or four of you, or five of you. He just makes lots of little copies of himself."

"So what do we do?"

"We make him attack someone *else*," Ryan said. "In the game, the Trow King isn't in a big ballroom place like this, but he is in a place called, I forget, the Trow Feasting Hall? Anyway, it's full of Trow sitting at long tables eating chicken legs and stuff. What you do is, you sneak in, grab some food off a plate, hide behind a trow, and throw food at the Trow King. Since he thinks one of his people threw it, he doesn't attack. He just starts shouting at them about how they'd better show him some respect. While he's yelling, you sneak over to another part of the room and throw another piece of food, so he'll think a different trow is hurling food at him. Do that three or four times, and the Trow King starts running around the room shouting at his people, stomping on tables all mad, and while he's distracted, *then* you sneak over and steal his treasure. Or, this time, his cup."

"That . . . sounds like a terrible plan," Silas said.

"Trust me." Ryan climbed out from under the table and looked at the food heaped on top. This table was all bread: dinner rolls, croissants, wheat, rye, sourdough, bagels, English muffins, challah, cinnamon buns, olive bread, focaccia, all kinds. He grabbed a handful of rolls, ducked under the table, and handed a few of them to Silas. "Okay. I'll go right, you go left, and we'll hit the Trow King. When he starts running around yelling, I'll grab the cup. Deal?"

"This seems ill advised," Silas said. "But I must admit, it also sounds fun." Silas scurried off into the crowd, quickly disappearing in the sea of inhuman legs. Ryan tried to play it cool, sauntering over toward a stubby-legged, short-armed, egg-shaped person so wide Ryan could have curled up in his stomach for a nap. He hurled a roll at the Trow King, then ducked behind the egg man's back without waiting to see if he'd made impact. Ryan played first base in Little League—he could hit a target as big as the Trow King from that distance, no problem. He saw another roll go flying at the same moment, sailing over the heads of the guests, and though it missed the Trow King, it bounced off the back of his chair next to his head.

The Trow King didn't rise from his chair, roaring. Instead he slumped, holding his head in his hands, and began to sob, his shoulders shaking. Ryan lowered his arm, still holding a dinner roll. He looked around for Silas, but

31

didn't see him, so he stepped tentatively toward the Trow King. So far, everyone in the hall was ignoring him, and Ryan was hesitant to call attention to himself, but . . . the Trow King was *crying.*

"Hi," Ryan said. "Are you okay?"

"They pelt me with stale crusts." The Trow King's voice was deep and mournful, and sounded sort of like rocks rattling around in an aluminum can. "Bad enough they laugh at me, but must they throw things at me too? I was a king among my people before the Horned Lord Herne brought me here as . . . as a decoration. It wouldn't be so bad, if they would let me dance and join their revels, but no one will dance with me. It makes me so angry!" His ears twitched, stiffening, but then sagged, and he slumped even further. "I was a mighty warrior. But fighting these elf knights and fairy ladies is like trying to fight smoke. I might as well try to wrestle the Boneless." He looked up, his watery eyes blinking at Ryan. "What are you?"

"Uh. Human?" Ryan said.

The Trow nodded, but seemed uncertain. "I've . . . heard of those. A kind of ape, aren't you?"

Ryan thought about that. "I guess you could put it that way. I'm a stranger here too. I'm sorry they won't let you dance."

"That's very kind of you," the Trow King said. "Be careful handing out kindnesses. I think fairies are allergic."

Silas sidled over. "Greetings, Trow King," he said formally. "I am Silas. I am also a captive of the fairies."

"Well met." The Trow King lifted his cup in a toast. He sipped, then grimaced. "Terrible," he said. "Everything I drink out of this cup tastes like it's been in someone else's mouth first. I don't know why Herne insisted on giving it to me. Another cruel joke, I suppose. It's probably poisoned."

Ryan glanced at Silas. "Could we . . . have the cup?"

The Trow King shrugged. "It's not mine. It belongs to the Horned Lord. But he's not here." He considered. "You may have it on one condition."

Ryan nodded. There were sometimes quests like this. Like you're supposed to go get a magic scroll from a druid, for instance, but the druid demands you give him an owl feather first, and the owl wants you to catch him a dozen mice and make mice soup, and you have to do three favors just to get the one thing you need. "What do you want us to do?"

"Dance with me," the Trow King said.

"I am willing, sir," Silas said. "But you are twice as tall as we are."

"Twice as tall, but there are *two* of you, so you may divide my height between you, and we'll be well matched." The Trow King's ears were lifting jauntily again.

"I don't understand . . ." Ryan began, but then he did, because the Trow King started to change.

In *WHO*, before he split into multiple versions of himself, the Trow King bellowed, "FISSION!" But he didn't say anything this time, just squeezed his eyes shut and appeared to concentrate very hard, his ears lifting until they pointed almost straight up, like a bat's. His tin crown fell off and hit the floor with a sad little tinkle. The Trow King grabbed the arms of his chair and grunted like . . . well, like Ryan's dad in the bathroom the day after chili night.

Silas stepped back, and Ryan did too, because this seemed a lot sweatier and messier than it was in the game—which made sense, as this Trow King was made of flesh, not pixels.

The Trow King slumped down on himself, and it was like looking at someone with your eyes crossed, all the vision doubled. He had two mouths, two sets of ears, four eyes, a pair of noses. Then it seemed like there were two boys trying to fight their way out of a bag made of gray elephant flesh, great bulges and ripples in the skin, and then two smaller Trow Kings began pulling themselves apart, long sticky strands like spit-strings connecting them. Finally they shook the last of the connective tissue loose and stood before Silas and Ryan, two Trow Kings each about four feet tall and quite moist. "I'll lead," the Trow King said in two simultaneous voices, and reached out for Ryan and Silas.

Silas acted like he'd done this a million times before, swooping off with his mini Trow King in a perfect graceful swirl. Maybe in the past, where he came from, since they didn't have *WHO* or TV or comics or skateboards or baseball or anything, they danced instead. But Ryan, who'd never done any dancing at all, unless you counted jumping around the living room while his dad played old rock music, didn't have any clue what to do.

Fortunately, the Trow King did. He grabbed Ryan's hands in his own and began gliding around the dance floor, dragging Ryan with him. The Trow King was strong—that much was like the game, even if nothing else was—and swung Ryan around like he was a doll. For his own part, Ryan just squeezed his eyes shut and tried to sway in the right direction in the faint hope that he might not get his arms ripped out of their sockets. He could hear a growing rumble of anger from the crowd of fairies, and he was certainly bumping into enough of the other dancers to cause a commotion. The Trow King was cackling as he danced, and he kept on laughing even after the music came to a jagged, jangling, screeching halt.

The Trow King put Ryan gently down, and when Ryan opened his eyes, he found he was standing right by the King's chair. "Your prize," he said, handing the cup to Ryan, who seized it with both hands—and it was a good thing too, because the cup was incredibly heavy. It swirled with impossible colors, and felt warm and slightly yielding in his hands—the texture was sort of like the slimy skin that forms on top of pudding, kind of interestingly nasty. The other half of the Trow King swooped in with Silas, who was grinning so wide it looked like it hurt his face—a real smile, finally. Ryan was beginning to think the fairies had stolen away his ability to smile.

But the smile faded as he looked around, and Ryan followed his gaze. The fairy revelers were all standing still, staring at the Trow King—fortunately, they didn't appear to be paying much attention to Silas and Ryan.

One of the Trow King's halves took a deep bow and shouted, "As you see, I dance better than any of you, even with untutored boys as my partners! Who'd like to have a lesson from me?" The fairies sneered at him, and a few booed, while others hissed. Hearing grown people—or things that looked mostly like grown people—hiss and boo was kind of ridiculous. Weren't they too old to do cheesy stuff like that?

The other Trow King leaned over to Ryan and whispered, "I'd go, now, before they start looking at *you*."

"Thanks, king," Ryan said. "We really appreciate it."

"I enjoyed the dance," the Trow King said. Ryan caught Silas's eye and jerked his head toward the door. They walked together along the tables, which suddenly didn't look so appetizing—the fruit was starting to smell bad, and flies were buzzing around the punch bowls, and the bread looked all moldy. Like the bad mood of the fairy revelers was affecting the quality of the refreshment. Well, maybe it did. This was fairyland. Fairyland was weird.

They'd made it almost to the door when the egg-shaped man stepped in front of them. He might as well have been a wall. He wore a green vest and shirt and coat and blue pants and pointy, shiny black shoes, but his clothes didn't completely cover his bulging roundness, and the skin underneath was whiter even than Silas and smooth as porcelain. He didn't have a neck, or even really a head—just a bulge at the top of his body where his tiny face was sort of smeared on.

"Thieves!" he shouted, his voice as high as a teakettle whistle. "They're stealing Herne's cup!"

"Uh oh," Ryan said. If the Trow King had been standing before him, or Tom Dockin, he would have ducked and darted between his legs and made it to safety. But the egg man had legs as short as a wiener dog's, so Ryan settled for kicking him in the shin. Of course, his leg was so short, kicking him in the shin was also pretty much kicking him in the knee and in the thigh, so the egg man howled and jumped away, hopping on one foot. "Come on!" Ryan shouted, and started racing for the door. The heavy cup seemed to squirm in his hands—now it felt like a newborn kitten, or a water balloon full of suspiciously warm liquid. The door was closed. *Why'd I shut it behind me?* Ryan thought—but Silas got to it faster and tried to yank it open. The egg man was still shouting, though more in anger than pain, and Ryan had the impression that a number of fairies were attempting to shove their way through the crowd to come after them.

"The door's stuck!" Silas yelled. "I think they've sealed it with magic!" He turned to look at the crowd, and his eyes went wide.

Ryan looked back too. Three of the tree-branch men were advancing, their sticklike fingers reaching out and flexing. The egg man stood on top of a table—one foot in a fruit bowl—and shouted, "As lord of this barrow, I command you to stop them! The little thieves are stealing what the Horned Lord stole first!" The floating instruments began to play an ominous, suspenseful, horror-movie sort of tune, and Ryan backed up against the wall, clutching the cup in his hands. "This isn't a game," he said, and it was only after he said it that it really got all the way through his mind: this wasn't a *game*. Silas had been trapped here a long time. The Trow King was trapped here. Even that jerk Gabriel Ratchet was trapped here. And now, the ones who'd kept them all prisoner were mad at *Ryan*.

Suddenly the fairies began to shout and flail and fall over, like pins knocked over by a bowling ball. Five, ten, fifteen—too many to count—mini Trow Kings appeared in the crowd, stomping insteps and kicking ankles and cackling. These little Trow Kings were no bigger than cats, but they seemed strong as superheroes, picking up fairies and tossing them left and right. None of the fairies seemed to get hurt—they just floated back down gently to the floor, like they were made of feathers, but they were certainly distracted and annoyed. One of the Trow Kings rushed the door, jumped up two feet, grabbed onto the handle, braced his tiny feet against the doorjamb, and pulled. The door popped open, and Silas and Ryan stepped toward it.

"Come with us!" Ryan said, but the little Trow King shook his head.

"Can't leave the party," he said. "It's forbidden."

"But—" Before Ryan could argue, Silas tugged on his jacket and pulled him back out into the barrowlands, under the sad sky. The tree-branch men were already kicking the mini Trow Kings aside and advancing on the door when Silas shut it in their faces—or, the sticks they had instead of faces.

"Quick, your shoe!" Silas yelled, and without asking why, Ryan tucked the fairy cup under his armpit, slipped his sneaker off, and handed it over.

Silas took a rusty nail as long as a pencil from his pocket and used the heel of Ryan's shoe to bang it into the doorframe, so it overlapped the door. Ryan couldn't really see the point—the door opened *inward*, so it wasn't like the nail would keep the door from working. One of the tree-branch men jerked the door open and started forward.

But stopped short before stepping through. The stick man didn't have eyes—or even a head, just a twig sticking up out of a collar—but Ryan could tell it was staring at the nail. Silas handed him back his shoe and began walking hurriedly toward the woods.

"Iron," Ryan said, hopping on one foot as he tried to put his shoe on and follow Silas at the same time. "It's iron! Fairies hate that stuff!"

"I have been holding onto that nail for a long time," Silas said. "I found it in the woods on my last free day and managed to sneak it in with me, I think, only because my captors were more interesting in laughing at Gabriel's attempt to escape than they were in searching me. I hate to give it up . . . but I was saving it for an emergency, and this was an emergency. We had better get back into the woods before the fairies have the sense to send one of their human servants to remove the nail."

"Won't they chase us into the woods?" Ryan said.

"I do not think so. The barrowlands, and the swamp, and the hills, and the forest, are all under the control of the Horned Lord, but their denizens do not often mingle. If the barrow fairies pursued us into the woods, they might find themselves pursued by worse things."

"Worse things." Ryan glanced at the branches hanging over them as they stepped back into the forest. "So isn't it dangerous for *us*?"

"A little," Silas said. "But not as dangerous as it would be for the barrow-folk. When humans fight amongst themselves, they don't go out of their way to kill the mice on the battlefield. As far as most of the fairies are concerned . . . we're mice."

Ryan grinned. "Some mice. Mice who stole their cup. How awesome was that?"

"Pretty awesome," the cup said. "That was really a close one, huh, guys? So where are we going now? I'm thirsty."

5

"YOU DIDN'T SAY THAT." RYAN PAUSED BENEATH A TREE.
"No," Silas said.

"The *cup* said it," Ryan said.

"That's right," the cup said.

Ryan put the cup down gently on the ground and took two steps away from it. "Are there a lot of talking cups in fairyland?" he said.

"Not in my experience," Silas said.

"Nor mine," the cup agreed. "So, are we going to get a drink?"

There were a few talking objects in *Wild Hunt Online*, and their example didn't fill Ryan with confidence. The only ones he knew about were talking swords, and they were all cursed. They told lies, and urged their wielders into dangerous situations, and claimed to have powers they didn't possess. Basically, in Ryan's experience, talking objects were pretty much all jerks.

"What do you like to drink?" Silas asked, being polite.

"Wine, cider, beer. Even mare's milk, in a pinch. Anything but water."

"What's wrong with water?" Ryan asked.

"Fish crap in it, for one thing," the cup said. "Listen, pick me up, would you? If you were going to leave on the ground, you might as well have left me with the Trow King. Lords and ladies, did *his* breath smell foul. Maybe fish crap in his mouth. That would explain a lot."

Silas, perhaps noting Ryan's hesitation, picked up the cup. "We did not know you had a voice," Silas said. "I apologize for taking you without your permission."

"No apology necessary. As I said, being the Trow King's drinking vessel was no pleasure cruise. I'm sure you boys will be much more fun. Where are we going? Another party?"

"No, we're going to—"

"Hold on," Ryan said. "Are you cursed?"

"Of *course* I'm cursed," the cup said. "Otherwise why would I be stuck in the form of a talking cup?"

"Wait. Someone cursed you and turned you into a cup? So you, personally, are cursed? You won't put a curse on *us*?"

"My boy, if I could curse anyone, it would be the Horned Lord Herne, who trapped me in this particular shape."

"Who were you before you were a cup?" Silas said. "If you don't mind me asking."

"What, you can't guess? What's 'cup' spelled backwards?"

"P, U, C," Ryan said. "Puck?" He whistled low. "Wait, *the* Puck? Like, Robin Goodfellow?" Puck (called Robin Goodfellow on the wanted posters) was a major figure in the world of *Wild Hunt Online*, not quite good and not quite evil, but a sort of trickster lord who ruled large swaths of the forest. Going through his territory was always a strange experience—step into the wrong spot and you could find yourself transformed into a horse, or a donkey, or a bunny rabbit. He also liked to lead people astray by appearing in disguise as powerful NPCs–non-player characters–or rare spawns, or even other player characters, beckoning and urging you to follow him to see something amazing. But the "something amazing" was usually a concealed pit filled with itchweed, or a swarm of angry dire bees, or just one of those trackless swamps, where your map stopped working and where walking in straight lines made you go around in circles.

"My legend precedes me, as well it should," Puck said, sounding pleased with himself.

"So 'Puck' backwards is 'cup', more or less," Silas said. "That is a very bad joke, but it still shows a greater sense of humor than I thought the Horned Lord possessed."

"Ah, well, as to that, it was my joke—and I don't think it's so bad, quite clever, actually. I'm a shapeshifter, you know, and one of my favorite tricks used to be disguising myself as a crab or a squab or a rabbit on a plate, and when a lady would pick me up for a bite or touch me with a fork, I'd start screaming, 'Please don't eat me!' Such fun! Ho! Ho! Ho!"

"Ho! Ho! Ho!" should have sounded harmless and Santa Claus–like, but somehow, coming from Puck, it was pure manic merriment. He continued in a more serious voice. "But that stopped being fun one night when an especially sour fairy matron went on poking me with her fork anyway—said she wasn't very well going to let dinner talk back to *her*. After that, I swore off taking edible forms. But I thought it would be the height of humor to disguise myself as a cup at the Horned Lord's table. *You* know what he's like—nothing amuses him, he takes himself more seriously than anyone should take anything, and he's got more dignity than a tree has leaves. So what could be funnier than pretending to be his cup, and then, when he picks me up for a drink, to spill my contents all down his front and into his lap? Ho! Ho! Ho!"

"Did it work?" Ryan said. "Was it funny?" He thought it sounded pretty funny.

"No one dared laugh," Puck said gloomily. "For the Horned Lord was so enraged. I could usually talk my way out of something like that, but he wasn't interested. He cast a spell of binding, trapped me in this form, and put me in a cupboard. After a while, it amused him to give me to the Trow King. The Horned Lord doesn't smile, but I think he was *thinking* about smiling when he handed me over to that beast."

"The Trow King was kind to us," Silas said. "You shouldn't say such cruel things."

"Oh. Hmm. Perhaps I should have given him a chance. Never even spoke to the fellow. Ah, well, the past is the past. Now, about that drink?"

"We should keep going." Ryan squinted through the branches at the sky above. The sun was up there somewhere, though he couldn't see exactly where. Surely it was lunchtime by now. Would his parents be mad if he didn't come home? Would they worry and search the woods? He hadn't brought his cell phone with him, and come to think of it, the thing probably wouldn't get service in fairyland anyway. "We don't want to run out of daylight before we run out of quest."

"A quest, is it?" Puck said. Silas kept the cup nestled to his chest as he set off through the trees again, leading the way. "For what, the holy grail? I'm not cup enough for you, is that it?"

"We must complete three tasks," Silas said. "The first was to steal you away from the barrowlands. The second is to dip you into the well of the moon—"

"Wait," Puck said. "Stop there. You want to put the water of the well of the moon in *me*? Don't you know what that stuff is supposed to do?"

"I understand it has many wonderful properties," Silas said.

"And you did say you were thirsty," Ryan pointed out. "I doubt any fish live in the well, so there shouldn't be any crap. Is the water poisoned or something?"

"Worse! So much worse! The first drink gives you wisdom! And the second drink gives you the curse of prophecy! Why would you wish such terrible things on your old friend Puck?"

"What's so bad about wisdom?" Ryan said.

"Oh, I suppose wisdom's all right, when you're too old to have any fun anyway," Puck said. "But the things I do, the things I *love*—wisdom would ruin them! Do *you* want to be wise?"

"Sure," Ryan said. "Knowing secret stuff sounds—"

"No, no, no," Puck said. "Wisdom isn't about *knowing* things. Wisdom is about knowing *better*. If you were wise, would you eat a whole bucket of Halloween candy and get so sick you threw up? Would a wise person watch scary movies even knowing they'd give him nightmares, or do something even more foolish, like dipping a girl's pigtails in an inkwell?"

"What's a scary movie?" Silas said, just as Ryan said, "What's an inkwell?"

Puck ignored them both. "No, forget wisdom. Give me foolishness every time. The wise don't have enough fun, and that's because they know better. May I never know better! And the gift of prophecy would be even worse, for all the same reasons. Knowing the future! What a terrible thing! Why, if I knew the consequences of the things I was going to do, I'd never do half of them. Do you think I would have played that prank on the Horned Lord of I'd known it would end with me stuck in the form of a cup for years and years, more or less kissing the king of the Trow on a regular basis? Of course not—and what a tragedy that would have been. The loss of a most hilarious practical joke. Wise Puck? Might as well have hot snow or dry water. I won't hear of it."

"I bet you'd like it," Ryan said. "It's wise to be wise, right? So once you were wise, you'd think it was a good idea."

"If *you* were wise," Puck said, "you wouldn't have taken on a quest that involved stealing me and annoying the Horned Lord. Think about *that* before you decide to poison me with wisdom."

"I am afraid we have no choice," Silas said. "You see, I must complete these tasks if I am to win my freedom."

"I see," Puck said. "I have some sympathy for the desire to be free. I suppose I don't have to *swallow* the water of the well of the moon."

"Don't!" Ryan said, alarmed. "The last task is to give the water to someone named Gentle Annie!"

"Ah. So I'm just to hold it in my mouth, then, for however long it takes you to transport me to this mysterious Annie? As if I, Robin Goodfellow, were little more than a common bucket?"

"That's pretty much the deal," Ryan said.

"Oh, all right then," Puck said. "It's not as if I have any choice. I'm a *cup*."

Silas stopped at the base of a thick tree, which was wrapped all over with vines as thick as Ryan's forearms. "This is the way to the well of the moon," he said, and Ryan looked around for a path or a tunnel or something. Silas shook his head and pointed up. "We climb."

Ryan frowned. "The well is up there? But . . . that doesn't make any sense!"

"Welcome to the neighborhood," Puck said.

"Can we fashion your jacket into some sort of sling to carry the cup—I am sorry, I mean Mr. Goodfellow—in?" Silas said. "I fear we will need both hands to climb."

Ryan shucked off his jacket, zipped it back up, tied the hood to one of the sleeves, and tied the other sleeve to the hem, making a sort of bag with a sleeve for an arm strap. They stowed the cup inside—Puck protested that he couldn't see anything, but he was muffled by the cloth, so Silas and Ryan pretended not to hear—and Ryan slung the improvised pack around his neck and under his arm, letting it hang on his back.

Silas went first, clambering up the tree effortlessly, and Ryan followed more slowly, checking his handholds and footholds carefully, the unfamiliar weight of the cup tugging toward the ground and throwing his balance off. They seemed to climb for a very long time, and when Ryan glanced down once, he couldn't see the ground at all, just a thick screen of branches, leaves the color of dying embers in a campfire. After that, he kept his eyes on the trunk ahead of him. At least if he fell, there would be a lot of branches to slow him down as he plunged toward his death.

He pulled himself up and found Silas sitting cross-legged, stretching his arms over his head and working kinks out of his neck. The branch where he sat was wide as a sidewalk, flat as a road, and extended off indefinitely. "This is the path," he said. "Come. We'll be there soon. I've only ever glimpsed the well from afar, and the women who guard it."

"There are guards?" Ryan said. "Of course there are guards. We should have taken more dinner rolls to throw at them."

"They're the daughters of a goddess," Puck said. "I wouldn't throw things at them, if I were you. Oh, wait, I forgot. My words of *wisdom* are wasted, because apparently the presence of an eighth of an inch of cloth renders me completely inaudible."

Silas walked along the path, and Ryan did too, albeit a lot more slowly, because there *was* the matter of the billion-zillion-foot drop on either side. But as he walked for longer, and the branch got gradually wider, he forgot about the drop, and it was a few minutes before he noticed they were no longer on a tree branch at all, but on a wide path strewn with bark fragments and wood chips, surrounded by forest. "Wait, we're back on the ground? But we never, like, angled back downward."

"We are still up in the treetops," Silas said. "Which is, it seems, the ground of some other place. I do not try to understand the geography of the Deep Woods—as long as I can find my way back the way I came, I am content."

At least Ryan could see the sun again, and amazingly, it still only seemed to be about noon, with the sun standing straight above him, making their shadows into puddles around their feet. Birds that looked sort of like crows swooped across the sky, but they faded in and out of visibility, vanishing in midair only to reappear some distance away, and a few turned from black to the puffy white of clouds as Ryan watched. They looked like birds, but they were obviously something else, or at least, something more.

The path meandered through low hills dotted with fire-colored bushes, and after a time Ryan thought he spotted something built, rather than growing wild, in the distance. "What's that up there?"

"I don't know, I can't *see*," Puck said peevishly.

Silas squinted and said, "It looks to be a well, my friend."

As they drew closer, they could see more clearly. Ryan had been imagining a wishing well, something with a little triangular roof and a bucket on a rope and pulley, but this was some older kind of well: a ring of stones about waist high, probably circling a deep hole in the ground. Three girls who looked a few years older than Ryan—in other words, babysitter-aged—lounged around the well: a blonde sitting on a tree stump squinting at a scroll, a redhead throwing rocks at the bizarre birds in the sky, and a brunette chewing on a strand of grass. They all wore pale gray robes—a bit grass-stained and dirt-smeared—and had the faces of pretty sisters.

"Visitors," the brunette said with a sigh, spitting out her piece of grass and plucking another one to chew instead.

"Intruders," said the redhead, tossing a baseball-sized rock up and down in her hand.

"Children," the blonde said, barely glancing up from her scroll.

"Hi there," Ryan said. "Is this the well of the moon?"

"No," the brunette said. "The well of the moon? Don't know where you got that idea. Guess you came all this way for nothing. You'd better move along."

"You really should," the blonde said, still reading. "Last time someone approached the well uninvited, my sister with the rocks there threw a bucket at him."

"Knocked him over like a little boy's sandcastle," the redhead said proudly.

"Of course, some of the well water in the bucket got into his mouth," the blonde continued, "giving him the gift of prophecy, and rather spoiling the whole point of the exercise."

"And what's the point of that again?" the brunette said. "It's a bloody great deep *well*. It's filled with water, and it's magical besides, so it's not like it will ever run out. Why don't we sell dippersful of the stuff? At least then we'd have money to buy something to eat."

"And something new to read," the blonde said. "I practically know this scroll by heart. But it's mother's well, and mother says we have to guard it, so."

"Get lost." The redhead threw a rock toward Ryan. She missed—he heard it whistle past his ear, but it was still a miss—though it was pretty clear she'd missed on purpose, and wouldn't necessarily miss the next time.

A muffled voice from within Ryan's bundled jacket said, "Boys, let me handle this—speaking to ladies is one of my specialties." He launched into a speech so flowery and full of funny old words that Ryan couldn't follow half of it, and the bits he could understand made him want to roll his eyes, gag, or blush, depending. The speech was about two-thirds flattery and one-third boasting, which, for Puck, probably counted as modesty.

When he was done, the blonde had a thoughtful look on her face, the brunette was gaping, and the redhead grinned. "You have a very eloquent jacket, there," she said. "But pretty words aren't much good to us." A crow swooped by, low, and she cursed and hurled a rock at it. The crow squawked when the rock clipped its wing, and flapped off in a fury, cursing in an almost-comprehensible language. The redhead went on. "Our mother, who is a goddess and therefore tricky to disobey, left us here to guard this well, with nothing to eat but dandelion greens, nothing to drink but dew—oh, no, we can't drink the *well* water, of course not—and all these stupid birds, which are not even proper birds but the *ghosts* of birds, crapping everywhere. Oh, and my sister only brought a few scrolls to read because she didn't realize we were going to be here *forever*, and she's pretty insufferable when she doesn't have new words flowing into her mind through her eyes. In short, we're fairly unhappy, and one of the only things that gives me any pleasure at all is throwing rocks at people who come too close to the well. And guess what? *You're too close to the well.*" She cocked back her arm and prepared to let loose another stone.

"Ryan, we'd better go," Silas said. "I knew our quest could not succeed."

"Yes, these women are hopeless," Puck said. "If I were in one of my non-cup forms, they would have been much more impressed, I'm sure, but given my current limitations—"

"Wait," Ryan said. "I've got an idea." He pulled his slingshot from his pocket, knelt to pick up a rock, and slipped it into the sling.

"Ryan, you can't *shoot* her," Silas said.

"Oh, you can *try*," the redhead said. "It's been ages since anyone fought *back*."

I hope this works, Ryan thought, and pulled back the slingshot, and fired.

6

RYAN WAS NO CRACK SHOT WITH A SLINGSHOT, BUT this time he hit was he was aiming for. One of the ghost crows squawked when the rock he'd fired thumped it in the side, and it fell in a shower of feathers, only to vanish from sight a foot before hitting the ground. All the well guardians stared at him, as did Silas, and Puck probably would have too, if he'd been able. Ryan flipped the slingshot over in his hand and held it out, handle first, toward the redhead. "You can hit a lot more birds with this. I'll give it to you if you let me get some water from the well."

"Deal," the redhead said, and snatched the weapon from his hands. She walked off, chortling, in the direction of a large pile of stones.

"Just because she'll let you pass doesn't mean *I* will," the brunette said, rising. "I haven't had a proper meal in ages, and being hungry puts me in a foul mood."

"I've got some trail mix," Ryan said, fishing the bag from his pocket. He was pretty hungry too, and hated to give up the only snack he'd brought with him, but this was an emergency.

The brunette stared at the bag in his hand. "Whose table is it from? What will eating it bind me to?"

Ryan shrugged. "My mom just goes through the bulk food aisle at the grocery stores and gets a bunch of dried fruit and stuff to mix it up. This is, let's see, dried pineapple and papaya, macadamia nuts, raisins, cashews—it's mom's tropical mix, with a handful of chocolate chips dumped in too."

"Food, freely given, with no obligation?" the brunette said.

"Well, not *no* obligation. You can have it if you let me take some water from the well," Ryan said.

"Agreed," she said, and pulled the bag away. She walked off too, stuffing a handful of fruit into her mouth.

The blonde sighed, rolled up her scroll, and stood. "And what will you offer me?"

"Um . . . Do you want my jacket?"

"I do not."

Ryan didn't want to fight, but it *was* two against one, now, so maybe Silas could get the water while Ryan tried to keep her distracted . . .

The blonde was shaking her head, and Ryan knew she'd figured out what he was thinking. "Don't think you can best me, young man. My sister is deadly accurate with her missiles, and my other sister fights with great ferocity, but some consider me the most dangerous of Beag's daughters. For you see, I have studied the old magics, and can bring down terrible beasts and summon a thousand causes for lamentation."

"All true," Puck said. "That's the blonde, right? She's wicked. You sure you don't have anything to trade her?"

Ryan's pockets were empty except for his house key and the coin Silas had given him, and he didn't think she'd want either of those. "I don't—" he began.

"Here." Silas pulled something from under his shirt. It was a comic book, folded in thirds, that he'd had shoved into the waistband of his pants. Ryan recognized it as one of the comics from the clubhouse. Silas looked at Ryan sheepishly. "I am sorry, my friend. I should not have taken it, but I was not finished reading it. I *had* intended to return it when I finished."

"Hey, you paid me," Ryan said. "Don't worry about it. I read that one already anyway." He looked at the blonde, whose eyes were focused intensely on the comic in Silas's hand. "It's really good," he said.

"Does it have philosophy in it?" she asked.

"Uh . . . Does guys in capes punching the snot out of each other count as philosophy?"

"Not even remotely," the blonde said. "May I read it?"

"If you let us get water from the well," Silas said.

"Agreed. Our bargain is struck." She took the comic from Silas and went off to join her feasting, crow-shooting sisters.

"Ryan," Silas said. "We *did* it. We can complete the second task!"

"Yeah! Now all we have to do is . . ." Ryan trailed off. "Oh, crap." He began to shake his head. He couldn't remember when he'd been so disappointed—maybe last Christmas, when his mother told him he wasn't getting a pair of real nunchucks and never, ever would, if she had anything to say about it. "We can't do it, Silas. We can't complete the quest."

"Why not?" Silas's voice was low and sad. Not arguing. More like he'd been expecting something like this all along.

"We have to climb back down the tree to get to Gentle Annie, right?" Ryan said.

"That's true."

Ryan spread his hands. "How are we supposed to fill a cup with water from the well of the moon and take it to Gentle Annie without spilling a drop when we have to *climb a tree*? Sticking the cup in my jacket isn't going to work again, and we can't make that climb one-handed. We'd spill everything. What are we going to do?"

Silas shook his head, and they both stared at the well for a while, and listened to the sisters laugh and chew and exclaim some little distance away. *My quest failed*, Ryan thought, *and I don't even get to eat any trail mix.*

"All right, fine, *fine*, I can't stand all this moping and silence," Puck said. "Dip me in the water, boys. I'll solve your problems for you."

"How?" Silas asked, reasonably enough.

"A genius doesn't go around revealing his methods to just anyone," Puck said. "It spoils the surprise. But you're a fairly appreciative audience, so: One of my favorite tricks while in cup form—or goblet form, or even a tankard, I'm versatile—was to wait until someone filled me with wine or beer, and then, before they could take a drink, I'd make the wine disappear . . . by swallowing it. They'd either think they'd lost their minds, or start yelling at the servants for not keeping their glass filled. And when they tried to refill the glass, I'd . . . Well, this is indelicate, but you might say I'd spit the wine back *out*, so when they poured another glassful, the cup was already full, so it would overflow and make a terrible mess. Ho! Ho! Ho!"

"You'd spit the wine back *up*? That's nasty." Ryan was torn between appreciation and disgust.

"Oh, well, it's not as if I have a proper stomach in this form anyway. It was more that I'd suck the wine into the stem of the goblet or into the handle of the tankard anyway. It's not as bad as it sounds. Dip me in the well and fill me up, and I'll suck the water down so you can carry me wherever we're going next without spilling."

"But won't that make you wise?" Silas said. "Swallowing the water?"

"I hope only temporarily," Puck said. "If I spit all the water back out again, perhaps the effects of wisdom will pass? And if not, well, there may be worse things than wisdom. Maybe if I'm wise I'll be able to figure out how to get out of this shape."

"We really appreciate this." Ryan untied his jacket and fished out the cup. "If we can do anything to help you with, you know, your problem, we will."

"Careful about promising favors," Puck said. "Fairies are touchy about that sort of thing. Let's get this over with."

Ryan carried the cup over to the well. He'd expected a deep dark shaft with maybe a glimmer of water at the bottom, but instead, the well was full almost to the top of the stone rim with clear, dark liquid. There was something strange about the water, and for a moment he couldn't figure it out. When he did, he whistled. "Silas, come look at this. What do you see when you look in the water?"

Silas peered over. "What do you mean? That's just the reflection of the moon—" He broke off, looked into the bright blue sky—which contained the sun and several ghost-birds and a few whizzing stones from the redhead's slingshot, but no moon—and then looked back at the water. "The well of the moon. It reflects the moon even when the moon isn't in the sky."

"It's actually much stranger than that," Puck said. "The water is suffused with moonlight, and in a way, the well is actually *on* the moon . . . But never mind that. Just dip me in. And be careful not to let any of this splash into your mouths, or *you* poor boys might become wise too, and then you'll never again be able to sit down and eat a whole container of jellybeans or jump off the roof of your house onto a trampoline."

Ryan pulled back his sleeves so they wouldn't get wet, and dipped the cup into the well, tilting it upward as he lifted it back out, so it was filled nearly to the top. As he watched, the water bubbled, a faint *glug-glug-glug* noise emerged from the cup, and the level of liquid fell until there was nothing left, not even a stray drop. He'd expected to see a little mouth open in the bottom of the cup or something, but Puck's magic was subtler than that.

"How do you feel?" Silas asked.

"Refreshed. Very tasty water, quite clean, with just a hint of moonbeams. I think its magical properties are vastly overstated—oh. Oh, my."

"What's wrong?" Ryan held the cup out at arm's length. If Puck had figured out how to turn back into himself, he didn't want the cup transforming into a full-grown fairy so close to his face.

"I just . . . Everything makes *sense* to me now. There are so many things I understand. Boys, listen. Boys. Are you listening?"

"We're listening," Silas said.

"It is better," Puck said, "to light a candle," Puck went on, "than to curse the darkness."

Ryan and Silas were silent for a moment. "I think I read that in a fortune cookie once," Ryan said.

"Listen, listen. I feel another one coming on. 'If you plant thorn bushes, don't walk around barefoot.' Eh? Good, isn't it? This wisdom is wonderful. Here's another: 'What is Buddha?' Don't know? The answer is 'three pounds of flax.'" Puck paused. "I expected more of a reaction from that. I'd hoped you two would fall to the ground, maybe roll around a bit, clap your hands to your eyes, and achieve enlightenment. Well, I have more, fear not. Why—"

Ryan bundled Puck back up in his jacket, wrapping him up more tightly this time, so the fairy's voice was more muffled. "Let's hurry to Gentle Annie's," Ryan said. "And hope this really *is* temporary."

Silas put his hand on Ryan's arm. "Do you really think we might succeed? That I might win my freedom?"

"Of course! You're practically free already. All that's left is the *easy* part— we just have to do a delivery. In *Wild Hunt Online*, the deliveries are the easiest quests of all. They're really just a way to move your character along when he's finished all the quests in one part of the Endless Forest. Some guy says, 'Here, deliver this letter to such-and-such a guy at such-and-such a place,' and when you get to the place, there are a bunch of new adventures waiting for you. Don't worry, Silas. The hard part's over."

"I hope so," Silas said. "But the fairies . . . Their ways are treacherous. They are often at their most dangerous when they seem the most harmless."

"Just because the water is calm!" Puck shouted from inside the bundle of cloth. "Doesn't mean there aren't any crocodiles!"

"Aren't wise people supposed to be quiet and think about the nature of the universe?" Ryan scowled. He didn't want Silas to get any more worried. The kid's life had been too hard—he deserved some happiness and confidence.

"Not when there are two youths such as yourselves in need of my tutelage!" Puck yelled.

"I don't even know what 'tootaledge' is," Ryan said. A rock whizzed by his head, and he spun around to see the daughters of Beag approaching.

"You dipped your water from the well," the blonde said, "in accordance with our bargain."

"Which means our bargain is done," the redhead said, pulling the slingshot back.

"Amb oar chespacking," the brunette said, her mouth stuffed with trail mix.

The blonde sighed. "Yes. As my sister said: And you're trespassing."

"Ladies!" Puck bellowed. "You catch more flies with honey than with vinegar!"

"We're going!" Ryan tucked the bundle of jacket and cup under his arm and backed away as quickly as he could, Silas beside him. The redhead had the pocket of the slingshot pulled all the way pack, and she had one eye shut as she took aim, her weapon tracking them as they moved away.

"They were nice boys," the blonde said. "Not like that awful fellow you threw the bucket at, sister."

"Ish tail icks ish delishush," the brunette said.

"Just give me a reason," the redhead said, but by then, Silas and Ryan were back on the path strewn with woodchips, hurrying toward the treetops again. The path gradually turned back into a broad branch instead, and though this time Ryan tried hard to pay attention, he still had a hard time pinpointing the exact moment the landscape went from low hills to treetops. The bushes along the path grew thicker, and then, without any fuss or fanfare, stopped being bushes and started being leafy tree branches instead. Puck kept on babbling the entire time, though being so tightly wrapped up and dangling from Ryan's back meant they couldn't quite understand anything he said— which wasn't so different from when they *could* hear him, after all.

They reached the central trunk, and Silas said, "Here, tie him on to my back—you had to climb up with him, so you deserve to descend unencumbered."

"You won't hear me argue." Ryan untangled himself from the jacket. "My mom always says you should refuse anything anybody offers you at least three times before accepting it, just to be polite, but I always think, what if they only ask you once? Makes more sense not to *offer* to do something unless you really want to, right?"

"Agreed. Though when dealing with fairies, refusing their offers is often the safest choice. You don't want to owe them favors. The only thing worse is when they think *they* owe *you* a favor. They go a little mad when they have an unpaid obligation, and can sometimes do terrible things to make it right again. If you let a fairy sleep on your porch, he might burn down your house in order to have the opportunity to give *you* a place to stay for a night. That's why I gave you that coin for the comic books—a long habit of paying off all debts." He pulled the strap of the jacket-sack over his neck and arranged the bundle. "Of course, some fairies give favors freely."

"Like the shoemaker's elves in the story, right?" Ryan said.

Silas nodded. "And there are others, especially brownies, who will attach themselves to a household and do all manner of chores. In return, they will take a little milk or bread, but you can never *offer* them the food—you just leave it out, as if you'd forgotten it, and the brownies will take it. If you offer payment, or to give them clothes, the brownies become horribly offended and leave forever." Silas shook his head. "Doing business with fairies is confusing." He looked around the trees thoughtfully. "I would quite like fairyland," he said, "if only there were no fairies. I love the magic of this place. But the ones who live here do their best to make it unpleasant."

"We'll get you out. There might not be as much magic back in my world, but if you've never seen a television or a car or a roller coaster or an ice cream store, I bet it'll seem pretty magical anyway. You want to go first, or should I?"

"I will go first," Silas decided. "That way if I drop this great heavy cup, it will not land on you." Silas clambered down the tree trunk, using the thick vines that encircled the tree for hand and footholds as easily as climbing down a ladder. Ryan went down after him, and it was a bit easier without Puck dangling off his back . . . but he still kept his eyes mostly on the trunk in front of him instead of peering down at the screen of branches and thinking about the ground far, far below.

As they neared the ground, they heard what sounded like . . .

"Cats?" Ryan said.

"Yes, I hear them too," Silas said. "A *lot* of cats."

Puck bellowed, "A cat may look at a king! Curiosity killed the cat, but satisfaction brought him back! The purity of a man's heart can be measured by how he regards cats!"

Ryan set his feet and paused in his climbing. "So, there are cats down there. Should we worry? Are there, I don't know, monster cats?"

"There is the Cait Sith, the fairy cat, as big as a dog, but . . . this sounds like a lot of normal-sized cats."

"So not the, whatever you said, Kate She then. Nothing else?"

"The only other supernatural cat I know of is a great monstrous one called Big Ears," Silas said, "but it would sound even less like normal cats, I think."

"There's a king of cats in *Wild Hunt Online* who just acts like a normal cat most of the time, but every so often he meets with hundreds of other cats in a clearing in the woods, and they can be pretty dangerous if you stumble across their meeting. But it doesn't sound like enough cats for *that*. Oh well. We can't stay in this tree forever, and cats can climb trees *anyway*, so even if they are dangerous, we're not safe."

Silas nodded and resumed climbing down, with Ryan following. Soon they were through the screen of branches, and Silas said, "Oh, no," in a quiet voice. Ryan looked down.

Gabriel Ratchet was waiting at the base of the tree, still perched on Tom

Dockin's shoulders. Cats were perched all over Tom's neck, arms, and shoulders, and Gabriel held a white cat in his arms, stroking it gently. They were all—even the cats—looking up the tree, and Gabriel was smiling.

"Those who play with cats," Puck shouted, "should expect to be scratched!"

After a still moment, Silas started climbing down again, and Ryan followed.

7

"MY FRIENDS!" GABRIEL SAID WHEN THEY DROPPED down to earth. "How goes your quest?"

"We're in the middle of it," Ryan said. "And we're pretty busy, so we'll talk to you later, okay?" Gabriel was the one speaking to them, but Ryan stared at Tom Dockin, who was just as hideous and scary as before, but also somehow ridiculous, with those cats clinging to his body, meowing away. There was a black tabby and a silver tabby, a Siamese, a white kitten, a Bombay, a calico, a Cornish Rex, and other kinds Ryan didn't recognize, about a dozen in all. The cats yawned and kneaded Tom's hairy flesh and licked themselves and generally did what cats do, not paying much attention to the fact that they were standing on a giant. For his part, Tom looked pretty miserable about it, and maybe even a little embarrassed.

"Ah, but don't you want to know how my plan to escape is going?" Gabriel scratched the white kitten in his arms behind the head.

"Of course," Silas said. "We wish you only the best."

Gabriel sighed. "The truth is, I don't think it's going to work. I can't find enough cats, you see."

Ryan was interested despite himself. "What do cats have to do with it?"

"Well you see," Gabriel said, "I went to old Black Annis the hag and said, 'All these little tricks you've taught me are well and good, but I want to *leave*. How can I get out of this place?' And she said that was beyond her power, but that there *were* forces in the universe that could grant me a wish. So I traded her the memories of all my birthdays—ha, come to think of it, I don't even remember when my birthday *is*, now—to learn the most fearsome magical spell she could teach. One so horrible even *she's* never done it. Only before we made the deal, she didn't tell me it required such a ridiculous quantity of *cats*."

"Not the Taghairm," Silas said, and from the horror in his voice, Ryan knew that must be something awful.

Gabriel brightened. "Ah, you know it? Your dear sainted mother must have told you about it, hmm?"

"She saw the rock," Silas said softly. "Where the demon appeared, the last time someone summoned it. She said you can still see the claw marks in the stone where it stood."

"Wait, there are demons now *too*?" Ryan said.

"There are more things in heaven and earth, Ryan," Gabriel said. "And other places too. Who can say if it's a demon? Maybe it's a small god, or a feral fairy. Apparently people call it Big Ears—like a silly name makes it any less dangerous. It's . . . a cat. Or a cat spirit. You can summon it, and when it appears, it will grant you a boon. They say summoning Big Ears dooms your soul forever, but I'm still young, and I bet there are ways to live forever so it's never a problem. But the problem *is*—not enough cats. You have to sacrifice cats, you see, lots of them, in a ritual that takes four or five days. I'm afraid I'd run out of cats long before I ran out of days. I made a lotion out of catnip and a little magic and smeared it on old Tom here, and that made him very attractive to all the cats in fairyland, but even though the beasts have an affinity for the place, there aren't *that* many hereabouts. I'd slip into the real world and go to a pet store, but I'm guessing an unattended thirteen-year-old boy asking to buy cats by the dozen would lead to certain awkward questions?"

"I think so," Ryan said. "You would really sacrifice *cats*?"

Gabriel snorted. "I grew up—before I came *here*—on a farm. My father used to put cats in a sack with rocks and toss them in a pond because we had too many. Cats are a renewable resource."

"You're sick," Ryan said. "They're alive. They have feelings—"

"And they die. Like every other living thing that has feelings. At least if they died in the course of my casting the Taghairm they'd die doing something to help *me*. But it looks like I won't be able to get my wish, not unless some of these cats fall in love and make me lots of little kittens. Which means my Plan A is at least delayed, and possibly canceled. That brings me to Plan B." Gabriel smiled brightly. "Which is: I steal *your* plan. So what is it, exactly?"

"Why should we tell you?" Ryan said.

Gabriel patted Tom Dockin on the head, and the giant grinned. His teeth were gray metal, and very sharp. "You may not have noticed, but I'm astride a *giant*. Not a very big giant, I know, compared to some, but big enough to make a meal of the two of you with room left over for dessert. So tell."

Silas sighed. "We had to steal a cup, from the barrowlands."

"Don't tell him!" Ryan said.

"Tom Dockin will eat us," Silas said. "I'd rather have Gabriel steal my chance at escape than be eaten by a giant."

Ryan could see the sense in that, but he didn't like it.

"Yes, you got the cup, and?" Gabriel said.

"Then we had to fill the cup at the well of the moon."

"Ridiculous. Beag's daughters are ferocious, even I've never been able to get close to them. I still have a scar on my arm where one of them threw a shoe at me. How did you do it?"

"We asked them nicely," Ryan said. "Maybe you should try that sometime, instead of being the world's biggest jerk."

"If I'm the world's biggest jerk," Gabriel said. "It is only because I stand on the shoulders of giants." He thumped Tom Dockin on top of the head. "And don't you forget it. All right. What happens next?"

"We take the cup to Gentle Annie, in the hills, and let her drink, and she'll show me how to escape fairyland."

"Mmm. Gentle Annie. I may have heard Black Annis mention her once or twice. Another witch. By all accounts, less powerful. Specializes in weather spells and wind magic."

"But it's worth a try, I suppose. Hand over the cup and I'll make Tom go hungry for another few hours."

Silas loosened the jacket around the cup. "This is it," he said.

Gabriel frowned. "It's *empty*. Did you fools spill all the water of the moon? It's more valuable than silver and gold, that stuff, I could trade it for—"

"It's not spilled," the cup said.

Gabriel leaned forward and peered down past Tom Dockin's nose. "Who is that speaking? I heard someone else yelling while you were coming down the tree, but I thought it was my ears playing tricks. What, do you have one of the little flower fairies nesting inside the cup? They get in everywhere. They're worse than moths—"

"I know that voice," Tom Dockin said, deep and mournful. "Ho. Ho. Ho."

"Surely not," Gabriel said. "No one has seen Puck in *ages*. They all say the Horned Lord did something terrible to him—"

"That's Robin Goodfellow to you, boy," the cup said. "Puck is what my friends call me. Perhaps you don't *know* this—but I'm extremely fond of cats. You might want to reconsider the way you speak to the people here who *are* my friends."

"Hmm," Gabriel said. "You're being a *cup*. Why are you being a cup?"

"To carry the water, stupid child. Water *you* could never acquire. These two boys together are braver and cleverer than you alone, Gabriel Ratchet. Best let them pass . . . before you upset me."

"If you're carrying water, where is it?"

"I swallowed it, to keep it safe," Puck said. "I can spit it back up when we get where we're going."

"Ha. You drank the water! So you're wise now, Puck? *You*?"

"That's Robin Goodfellow" Tom rumbled, "even if it looks like a cup. I don't like him. He plays tricks. He's fast. He's smart. And now he's wise? Don't trouble him, Gabriel Ratchet. He was old when you were nothing at all."

"Thus proving even great stupid giants sometimes speak the truth," Puck said. "Stand aside. Stealing me won't do any good. I wouldn't spit the water back up for *you*, so you'd just be barging into a witch's cave, promising great gifts you can't deliver."

"Hmm." Gabriel stroked the cat behind the ears and looked off into the middle distance for a while. "Yes, I see your point. There are ways I could try to force your hand, extort your help, but you're *Puck*, and your reputation precedes you. I know you're a difficult creature to beat in a test of wits, and if you're wise now too . . . I know when I'm beaten. Carry on. Best of luck to you, Silas. I'll miss seeing your wretched, snotty, dirt-smeared little face around here. Come, Tom. Let's get started on Plan C." The giant stomped off, cats yowling as they dug in their claws to keep their footing while he moved.

"That's *it*?" Ryan said. "He's just giving up?"

"I doubt it," Silas said. "But he's not going to feed us to Tom and steal the cup. Thank you, Puck."

"Wisdom is not all pithy sayings and proverbs and koans, my friends," the cup said. "I have a fearsome reputation—entirely deserved—and I knew Gabriel would retreat rather than try to fight me directly." Puck paused. "Of course, it helps that he doesn't realize I'm trapped in cup form. It's not the most intimidating shape I've ever taken, I'm afraid. We'd best hurry to finish your quest before Gabriel comes up with another plan of attack."

They wrapped the cup back up and struck off through the forest. "Is it far?" Ryan asked.

"No," Silas said, lifting aside a branch and letting Ryan step through . . .

Into a swamp. Trees slimy with black moss grew out of dark standing water. Mist floated low along the damp—often liquid—ground, and a million frogs croaked dolefully. "I wouldn't mind some magic to keep my feet dry," Ryan said. He'd tromped through the swamps many times in *WHO*, but his avatar on screen didn't have real feet to get all slimy and damp.

"There's a sort of path." Silas pointed to a hump of grass. "You can hop from grassy patch to stump to grassy patch. Anywhere grass grows, the ground is probably solid enough to step on. Patches of moss might just be floating, and clumps of leaves too, but grass is a good sign."

"Anything dangerous in the swamp?" Ryan hopped after Silas, trying to put his feet exactly where his friend did. In *WHO*, the swamp was home to wicked hags, terrible swamp monsters composed of rotting vegetation, hungry frogs the size of barrels, leeches that could suck out your life force, shapeshifting horses called kelpies that would try to drown you, and other hazards.

"Once, after a trip to the swamp, a disgusting fungus began growing on my foot," Silas said. "And there is sometimes swamp gas that smells so bad it seems like something died nearby, and the stink can cling to you. But the only real danger is the will-o'-the-wisps, floating lights that try to lead you astray, but they do not attack directly. They prey on lost travelers and lead them to their dooms."

"Why do they do that?"

"I am not sure," Silas said. "To amuse themselves? Perhaps they feed on death, somehow? I am not even sure if they have minds."

"That is a mystery unanswered even by great thinkers like myself," Puck agreed. "I'm trying desperately to think of some wise words or parables relating to swamps, but really, I'm not coming up with much . . . Ah, here's one: 'When you're up to your butt in alligators, it's hard to remember you were trying to drain the swamp.'"

"Thanks, Puck," Ryan said. "That's really helpful. Now I'm worried about alligators."

"How about, 'Where there are no swamps there are no frogs?'"

"That is probably true," Silas said. "Except for all the frogs that live in places other than swamps."

"Tree frogs," Ryan offered. "And there are frogs that live in deserts. Or toads anyway."

"Quite right," Puck said. "Back to the drawing board with that one, eh?"

"So no Jenny Greenteeth or, what was the other one?"

"Nellie Longarms. No, they live in ponds and lakes and rivers. Or so my mother told me. I avoid such bodies of water, and have thus avoided them."

This place was so strange. Ryan couldn't figure it out. It was like a fairyland composed equally of things Silas's mother had warned him about as a little kid—probably just bogeyman stories to scare him into eating his vegetables, lots of parents had made up stories like that in the old days—and things Ryan knew from *Wild Hunt Online* and the little bit of related reading his mother had gotten him to do. And Silas had never seen the goblin men at the market or Ghillie Dhu or the Trow King before Ryan got here—he'd never even *heard* of them. Something about that tickled at the back of Ryan's mind, some possible explanation for why this place was the way it was. It had something to do with dreams, he thought, but this definitely wasn't a dream. Your sneakers didn't get so muddy and your legs didn't get so tired from walking in dreams, so . . .

"The hills." Silas hopped to another patch of grass, and from there it was *all* grass, moving into hills. But these weren't the gentle, rolling, partly artificial hills of the barrowlands; these were steep and stony hills, with sharp spurs of rock sticking up out of the grass like the broken bones of the Earth jutting through skin. Boulders as big as cars—some as big as houses—nested in the valleys between hills, and Ryan was soon breathing hard as they clambered over the uneven ground. As usual, Silas was agile as a mountain goat. *Maybe I should run around in the woods more*, Ryan thought. *Playing so much* WHO *is good for leveling my character up, but not so good for leveling* me *up.*

"That is the cave of Black Annis." Silas pointed to a dark hole in the side of one particularly jagged hill, some distance away. Smoke trickled out of the cave and streamed into the sky, and a huge gnarled oak tree grew halfway across the opening. "I have never been inside, though I have glimpsed the blue-faced hag on occasion. She does not eat people, as Tom Dockin does, but she eats memories. My memories are all I have left of my old life, and they are faded enough already by time."

"Why does she want to eat memories? What does that even mean?"

"She takes the things you remember," Silas said, "and you no longer remember them. They become her memories instead. Fairies are cruel, but they have no *imagination*. What is a memory but an imagining of the past? I think, when she steals your recollections, she steals a bit of your imagination too. That is why Gabriel Ratchet is so dangerous, I think: he combines the cruelty of fairies with human creativity."

Imagination, Ryan thought. *Imagination and dreams. What do those things have to do with* this *place?*

"There is some truth in what you say," Puck said. "But I wouldn't say we're *entirely* without imagination. Some of my pranks show quite a bit of cleverness, wouldn't you say?"

"Perhaps 'imagination' is the wrong word," Silas said. "Fairies can be very clever, it is true, and I mean you no offense, dear Puck, but . . . fairies do not create. They change things. They shape things. They even shape *themselves*, but they do not make new things. They do not write songs or poems, though they can be excellent singers and orators. Do you see the distinction?"

"I do, and wisdom prevents me from arguing with you," Puck said gloomily. "I hope this is just a temporary condition. I miss being my old self."

"We shall soon find out," Silas said. "I think the cave of Gentle Annie is on the other side of this hill." Ryan followed him past another scattering of stones and over a rocky hill, down the other side, and then along one of the little valleys for a while. A clear stream trickled through, and Ryan paused to sip from his water bottle when Silas bent to drink from the stream. He didn't have much water left in the bottle, and he didn't dare refill it—Silas could drink water from the fairylands, since he was already a prisoner, but Ryan couldn't take the risk. Silas said he couldn't be trapped here unless he ate or drank or accepted fairy hospitality or *asked* to stay. But he'd have to go home soon for more food and water. With luck, Silas would be going with him, free of fairyland forever.

"The cave." This place was the twin of Black Annis's lair, complete with an oak tree, though it leaned in the opposite direction, and no smoke poured out of the cave's mouth. Instead, a gentle breeze blew through.

"She's some kind of . . . wind witch?" Ryan said.

"So I understand," Silas said.

"She causes gales," Puck said. "Great gusts of wind that blow through the cracks in the hills. In this country, a storm can blow up on you suddenly— the shelter of a hill will suddenly become a wall the winds of a storm batter you against." He cleared his throat—quite a trick, since he didn't *have* a throat, and said, as if it pained him, "Her habit of calling up such storms gives her a bit of a reputation for treachery, I'm afraid."

"We have come this far," Silas said. "We should finish." He turned to Ryan. "Whatever happens, I want to thank you for doing so much on my behalf. You are the first true friend I have made in more than a century."

"I still say I get the better part of the deal," Ryan said. "I've seen goblin men and fairy revels, climbed trees into a world in the sky, outsmarted the daughters of a goddess—and I thought today was going to be *boring*. I just hope it works."

Silas stepped toward the cave opening. "Gentle Annie!" he called. "I come on a quest set for me by Ghillie Dhu, bearing a cup that holds the water of the well of the moon!"

The breeze stiffened and a small woman in a gray dress emerged from the darkness, her long dark hair blowing around her face, obscuring her features.

Something closed around Ryan's chest, and he was lifted into the air. He squawked in alarm, and Silas turned, gaping. Ryan looked up into the face of Tom Dockin, who held him wrapped in his arms. Tom opened his mouth and slowly moved Ryan's head up, until the cold iron of his upper row of teeth touched the top of Ryan's head.

Ryan squeezed his eyes shut, his mind an incoherent babble of terror, and waited for Tom Dockin to bite down... but nothing happened. So Ryan opened one eye, and saw Gabriel Ratchet come sliding down the side of the witch's hill. "Hello, everyone," he said when he hit the ground, not even stumbling. "Silas, ask the witch to free me from fairyland, will you?"

Silas stared. "I... You... You can't..."

Gabriel yawned. "Of course I can. It's simple. Have the witch set me free, instead of you, or I'll let Tom take a bite of your friend's head."

Something cold and wet slithered down the side of Ryan's face, and he realized Tom Dockin was drooling.

8

GABRIEL WENT ON. "SET ME FREE INSTEAD, AND I'LL MAKE Tom let him go. Or you can just complete your quest and win your freedom—after all, you don't *need* Ryan anymore, right?"

"He is my friend," Silas said, without hesitation. "Of course I will save him. Puck, return the water, so I may complete this quest."

"Silas, you've come so far. You shouldn't let yourself be bullied by this human brat—"

"Please," Silas said.

"All right. All right." There was a slosh and gurgle, and Silas stepped toward Gentle Annie—who'd stood without any comment throughout the previous exchange—holding out the cup. "This water is for you. All I ask in return is that you free Gabriel Ratchet from his captivity."

"Good boy," Gabriel said.

Gentle Annie took the cup in both hands, lifted it to her face . . . then turned it over, pouring the water out upon the ground. She dropped the cup—Puck squawked—and pushed her hair back with her hands.

Her face was old, sharp, and pale blue. She grinned, and her teeth were numerous and very sharp. "Boo," she said, and began to laugh.

"Black Annis," Gabriel said wearily. "This is what you do with the imagination you've stolen from me? Contrive tricks to play on Silas and his mortal friend? I've wasted half my free day on this nonsense." He gestured. "Tom, drop Ryan. We may need him later."

Tom Dockin growled, and for a moment, Ryan thought he was going to bite down anyway . . . but the giant's pledge to serve Gabriel was apparently stronger. He put Ryan down gently, and Ryan scrubbed at the top of his head to wipe the saliva away as he scurried toward Silas.

"There is no Gentle Annie at all." Silas lowered himself to the ground and sat down.

"Not exactly," Black Annis said. Her voice was harsh as the cawing of ghost crows. "My cave runs all the way through the hill. On one side, I'm Black Annis; on the other, I'm Gentle Annie. We used to be sisters, but after a while there weren't enough bodies to go around, so we share this one. She's no nicer than I am, though. But this joke wasn't *my* idea, young Gabriel. It came from a higher level."

Silas stood up, and Ryan could sense the tension vibrating through his friend. "What is it?" he said, but Silas just shook his head.

Gabriel said a dirty word and climbed up on Tom's back. "Let's get out of here, giant. I only know one thing who can give Black Annis orders." Tom Dockin loped away as if he were afraid too.

"You thought you could escape." The voice was deep, and booming, and emerged from the dark of the cave. "You, Silas. And you, Puck—foolish Puck. Or are you still wise? It does not matter—either way, it's back to the cupboard for you. But I'm curious."

"No, I'm entirely a fool again," Puck said cheerfully. "Got all that nasty water out of my system, so I'm foolish enough to trouble you until the end of your days."

"My days . . . do not end."

The Horned Lord Herne stepped from the shadows of the cave. He looked like a man with a black beard, but he was taller than the oak tree, dressed in strange pale leather with a curving horn at his belt, with a helmet on his head that bore the enormous antlers of a stag. Except Ryan couldn't see where the helmet *was*, exactly. It was almost like the horns were just growing out of his head instead—and then Herne flickered, and instead of a bearded hunstman, he was a faceless giant in a great black helm that entirely covered his face, with triangular eye slits, and topped with a huge rack of sharpened steel antlers. His armor was black plate mail, worked with a motif of thorns and branches, and the horn at his belt was banded in black metal. Smoke rose from the joints in the armor where the iron burned Herne's fairy flesh, but the Horned Lord bore the pain, and his long years in the armor made him immune to the bite of iron weapons that could easily kill lesser fairies. *This* was the Herne who adorned the cover of the box the *Wild Hunt Online* game discs came in, the most powerful boss in all of the Endless Forest.

He flickered back to the bearded huntsman shape, seemingly unaware of his own transformations. "You can never escape me, Silas. As long as I reign in the Deep Woods, you *will* be my prisoner." He smiled. "And now, boy, both of you boys, follow Gabriel's example, and *run*."

"You don't scare us—" Ryan began, but then Herne took the horn from his belt and put it to his lips.

"RUN!" Silas shouted, and set off at a gallop. Ryan had sense enough to follow him, terror restoring all the energy his long day of questing had used up. The horn blew, a long, low note, and then Ryan heard the baying of countless hounds.

Herne had summoned the Wild Hunt. There was no more fearsome thing in the Endless Forest. In the game, the Hunt appeared at random, racing through the forest, and if it came too close to you, you were either chased down and killed, or—and this was even worse—swept up in the madness and forced to join the hunt, your character taken out of your control, using up your best ammunition and potions and magic as you helped the Hunt chase down its prey, which was essentially anything that moved.

Silas raced ahead of him, back through the swamp, and the baying of the hounds grew louder, but Ryan didn't dare look back. They burst out of the swamp into the forest, and still Silas ran, leaping over fallen trees, vaulting over streams, darting between tree trunks that seemed too narrow for him to pass through . . . and Ryan followed on his heels, his heart thumping like a thousand drums, a painful stitch in his side from too much running, sucking down great breaths of air with every other step.

Until the baying of the hounds behind them abruptly stopped as they reached the familiar trees behind Ryan's house, not far from the clubhouse. Silas stopped running, bent over at the waist, and gasped—the first sign of exertion Ryan had seen in him. For his part, Ryan fell over in the leaves and just lay there for a while, breathing in the smell of the forest—the air was colder here, crisper, somehow more real and wide open.

After a while he rolled over. "Wow," he said. Silas, sprawled on his back in the leaves, grunted. "That was . . . I'm so sorry, Silas. I really thought the quest would work."

"I dared hope, briefly," he said. "But I knew, in my heart, that the Horned Lord would never let me escape so easily."

"I didn't think it was all that easy," Ryan said. "In the game—"

"This is not a game," Silas said quietly. "I allowed myself, for a while, to pretend it was—and I am not angry with you. I am grateful. Hope is something I seldom experience, and even the pretense of hope is pleasant. But now . . . I should return to my life."

"But what about the hounds?"

Silas shook his head. "The Horned Lord has set them on me before. He likes to watch me run. Do you think if he truly *wanted* to catch us we would have escaped? Herne's power is absolute. We just . . . amuse him." He stood up, brushing the leaves from his body. "Thank you for a morning that was more pleasant than not, my friend. I should return to my world, and you should stay in yours, where you will be safe."

"But, look, if Herne is the problem, then we just have to find a way to beat Herne—"

"Defeat the Horned Lord? You may as well try to knock the moon out of the sky with a slingshot," Silas said, "and you no longer even have a slingshot. No, Ryan. You have done enough, and risked enough. Tom Dockin had your head in his mouth. I would not put you in such danger again. Goodbye, my friend." He held out his hand, and Ryan shook it, trying to think of the words he could say to make Silas change his mind, to try again, to *keep* trying.

"Rye-uhn! Rye-uhn!" That was Ryan's mother's voice, faint but audible, calling him from the back porch. Which meant it must be lunchtime. Which meant that whole quest had taken no more than a few hours. It seemed impossible. But time could be funny in fairyland.

"At least come have lunch with me," Ryan said. "You've still got your liberty. I'll tell my mom you're a friend from school. I'll—"

"I could not bear it. To see what you have and what I cannot have . . . No. Go to your family." Silas's voice broke on the last word, and then he ran into the trees and disappeared, stepping back into the Deep Woods.

Ryan's mom stopped calling. She probably figured he was too far off to hear her. She wouldn't worry, as long as he showed up sometime soon. With some effort, Ryan dragged himself back up into the clubhouse and stared at the sky. He'd touched magic today . . . and magic had beaten the crap out of him as a result. Ryan knew there were some fights you couldn't win—in the game *and* in real life, and obviously in whatever fairyland was—but it still made him angry. Herne was ancient and powerful and a total jerk, and Silas would have to deal with his crap *forever*. And if Silas only got to leave the forest and spend a day in the real world every twenty or thirty years, Ryan would probably never see him again, unless he decided to come back here when he was all old and grown, to say hello, and what good would *that* do? Finally his hunger overcame his brooding, at least enough to send him back down the tree and trudging toward home. He was out of the forest in what seemed like mere moments, as if the woods had gotten smaller after his time in fairyland. He ducked under the old clothesline, walked past the woodpile, and paused by the rusty swing set. This was the real world, all right. And he was stuck here now. He'd failed, and his guide had left him behind, and the borders of the Deep Woods were closed to him.

Ryan's stomach rumbled, and he continued home, up the steps to the back porch, through into the kitchen. His mother was at the sink, washing up plates. "I'm starving," he said, climbing onto the stool at the breakfast bar.

His mother turned and looked at him quizzically. "Really, still? I guess you *were* out tromping in the woods all morning. There's some macaroni and cheese left, and I think a few fish sticks. Help yourself."

Ryan walked over to the stove. The fish sticks were cold, and the macaroni and cheese wasn't much better, but at least it was the kind made with cheese squeezed out of a silver packet and not with orange powder. Still, it was kind of crappy of his mom and dad to eat his lunch just because he didn't get home fast enough—they were usually nicer than that. He climbed back onto the stool and munched thoughtfully.

Herne, Herne, Herne, he thought. Herne was the problem. If fairyland was a prison, he was the warden. If only there were some way to beat him . . . "Hey, Mom, you've beaten Herne the Hunter, right?"

"Yep," she said, not turning around from the sink. "Our group was only the third one on the server to down him. We wiped about twenty times before we managed to beat him, though."

"How'd you do it?"

She turned around, wiping her hands on a dishtowel, and leaned against the sink. Her pale blue eyes took on a faraway look, and she didn't look at Ryan so much as past him. "You want to hear my war stories? It's a pretty tricky fight, actually . . . You know how, when the Wild Hunt appears, there's a chance you'll be swept up by the pack?"

Ryan nodded.

"It's a kind of charm spell, a compulsion. As soon as you enter Herne's wood, at the center of the Endless Forest—though really, if it's endless, how can it have a center?—one member of your party is instantly mind-controlled by Herne. That person is out of commission for the whole battle—and if it's your main healer, or your tank, someone really indispensable? Forget it. The mind-controlled member of your group starts attacking you, and you have to defeat them before you can even get close to Herne. Then he blows his horn and unleashes his hounds on you, dozens of mobs swarming all at once. You have to beat them, and then, without even a moment's rest, Herne blows his horn a second time . . . and everything you've ever killed in your entire time in the game comes back as a ghost and attacks you."

"Whoa," Ryan said.

His mom nodded. "It's pretty impressive, how the game keeps track of your kills, and everyone sees different ghosts on their screen. Fortunately they're not too tough. They're a lot weaker than they were when they were alive, but for most people, there are so *many* of them, it's brutal. After the ghosts are gone, Herne comes down from his throne of thorns and fights you directly. That's a pretty straightforward fight, though it takes forever to damage his armor. Eventually, when you get him down to about ten percent of his total health, you knock his helmet off—and then there's a cutscene movie that tells you the true origin of Herne." She paused. "I'd tell you about it, but it's a pretty big spoiler."

Ryan rolled his eyes. "It'll be like a *year* before I'm a high enough level to even get close to Herne's wood. Tell me! I don't care about spoilers."

"Just like your father," she said. "He always says spoilers don't matter, and that anticipation is a more sophisticated pleasure than surprise. He says, does knowing how *Romeo and Juliet* or *A Midsummer Night's Dream* end make them any less enjoyable? I think—"

"Mom! No Shakespeare! The game!"

She laughed. "Now, now—Herne comes from Shakespeare too, though there were legends about him before the Bard wrote about him. After you knock Herne's helmet off, you find out he's a human. Not a fairy at all, at least not originally. It turns out he was just a man once, who worked for a king as a hunter. One day he saved the king from being gored to death by a boar, but almost died himself. The king's wizard—actually a fairy—was ordered to save Herne's life, and he did, but he had to use fairy magic to do so, and Herne became part fairy himself in the process—that's why iron hurts him, but doesn't kill him, as it does true fairies. The king was very happy with Herne, and gave him great rewards, but the fairy wizard grew jealous and told lies about Herne to get him in trouble with the king. Herne was sentenced to death for crimes he didn't commit, and hung from an oak tree . . . but he escaped, using his fairy magic. He disappeared into fairyland, into the Endless Forest, and vowed to become a king himself in that world, so he wouldn't have to depend on anyone—fairies *or* kings—for help ever again. Of course, he becomes a bad king. Anyone with too much power does, but Herne combines the worst qualities of fairies and humans—"

"Cruelty," Ryan murmured, "and imagination."

His mom blinked. "That's very well put, Ryan. All those books I made you read must be rubbing off on you."

"I think I'm going to go back out," he said. "To the woods. For a while."

"That's what you said half an hour ago, the *first* time you had lunch," she said, "before you went to talk to your dad." She took his empty dishes away. "It's not nice making your poor elderly mother wash *two* plates and bowls, you know. Don't come back for thirds, either. Kitchen's closed."

"But I . . . " Ryan fell silent. "Sorry, Mom," he said, but it was as if he were hearing his own voice from very far away. He slid off the barstool, went through the door to the dining room, and crept down the hall to his parents' office, where his dad was playing *WHO*. He heard voices as he approached: his dad's and someone else's.

Ryan peeked around the doorjamb into the office. His dad was there, playing . . . and a boy was beside him. A boy with hair the same blond as Ryan's, wearing the same hoodie, the same jeans, the same sneakers. Pointing at the screen and laughing Ryan's laugh. And if he were to turn around, Ryan was sure he'd see the boy was wearing Ryan's own face.

He walked toward the den, hurrying as fast as he could while remaining perfectly silent, and snatched up a fireplace poker from the hearth. Cold iron. He slipped out the side door, which no one ever used, and hurried to the woodpile. After a moment's thought, he picked up the axe, but it was too heavy, and only the head was iron, not the whole thing. Ryan was worried he'd chop his own foot off if he tried to hit someone with it. He crouched down behind the woodpile, poker in hand, and waited.

After a few minutes, the back door slammed, and the boy wearing his face appeared, hopping down the steps and whistling. As he got closer to the woods, his face began to melt and run like melting candlewax, and he swiped at his cheeks and nose as if wiping sweat away. Underneath was the face of Gabriel Ratchet.

9

GABRIEL PAUSED BEFORE REACHING THE WOODPILE. "I know you're there," he said, wiping the last of the waxy stuff from his forehead. "Are you impressed by my glamour? Not as elegant as the illusions fairies can naturally cast, but more durable in its way. I fooled both your parents."

Ryan stood up with the poker in his hands. "What were you doing in my house?"

"Practicing. Not that I'll need a lot of practice to be you. 'Mom, I'm hungry! Dad, I want to play on the computer!'" His voice was different, higher-pitched, and though it didn't sound to Ryan's ears like his own voice, he guessed it probably sounded like a perfect imitation to others.

"You can't be me." Ryan stepped around the woodpile, holding the poker cocked like a baseball bat. "*I'm* me."

"For the moment. When your quest turned out to be nonsense, and I failed to acquire the necessary quantity of cats to cast the Taghairm, I thought up a plan C to escape fairyland. I'll just take over *your* life."

"When the day ends, you'll be sucked back into fairyland, just like last time, when you tried to hitchhike your way to freedom."

"Someone's been telling tales about me. You're right, of course; I can't just club you over the head and go live in your house. That's why I'm off to see Herne the hunter, and offer him a trade: my life for yours."

Ryan gritted his teeth. "Silas said I can't be trapped in fairyland unless I eat or drink something, or ask to stay, or accept hospitality."

"Those are the rules, yes. But they're only some of the rules. Sometimes children are stolen away and replaced by exact replicas, called changelings. Now, usually it's babies who are stolen, but I'm confident I can convince the Horned Lord to make an exception in your case—you're basically a baby, anyway, at least compared to Silas and me. I know we look like children, but he's well over a century old, and I'd be qualified for retirement myself, by calendar time."

"Why would Herne trade you for me?"

"Children are useful to him because of our imaginations, and I've been selling pieces of mine to Black Annis. Yours is all ripe and fresh and full." Gabriel shrugged. "It's a good deal. The Horned Lord will take it. Don't worry. Your parents will love me. I'll do better in school than you do, I'm sure, and make something of myself when I grow up—more than you ever would, anyway. Best get used to it. I'll be back to drag you into the Deep Woods later. Goodbye."

Ryan stepped in front of him, still holding the poker but unwilling to actually hit another human being with it . . . even when that human was Gabriel. "I won't let you, I *won't*."

"How will you stop me? I'm not about to escort you into the Deep Woods, and Silas is off sulking. You're stuck in the real world, and I'm . . . not." He sprinted for the trees, and Ryan ran after him, weapon in hand. He *had* to catch Gabriel before he made it back into fairyland, had to stop him before he could steal Ryan's life away. Gabriel wasn't as fast and surefooted in the woods as Silas was, and Ryan stayed right on his heels, but not quite within grabbing distance.

Gabriel looked back, laughed, jumped over a fallen tree, and vanished.

Ryan's heart sank, but momentum carried him forward, so he jumped over the tree too . . . and there was Gabriel, leaning against a tree and panting. His eyes widened when he saw Ryan, and he said, "*How?*" just as Ryan swung his poker.

Gabriel jumped out of the way, and Ryan's poker took a few chips of bark off the tree when it struck. "Did you eat or drink something here?" Gabriel said. "Damn it, if you're already trapped, it spoils my whole plan—"

"No, I didn't." Ryan struck out again, and Gabriel darted around another tree.

"Did Silas give you something? A key, a map—"

Ryan stopped. "He gave me a coin. Said he was paying a debt to me."

"A token of passage," Gabriel said. He exhaled. "That's a relief. It allows you to pass from your world to the fairy world . . . but only while the borders are down, today. Tomorrow it'll be just a bit of old metal."

"Why didn't Silas tell me the coin could do that?"

Gabriel shrugged. "He probably didn't know, but I've made a study of fairy magic. Which is why you shouldn't try to hit me with a metal bar. I have resources, you see." He put two fingers in his mouth and whistled, and the giant Tom Dockin lumbered out of the trees, as if he'd been standing around waiting to be summoned.

Ryan didn't hesitate—this was what he'd brought the fireplace poker for, and he had no qualms about attacking a giant. He swung as hard as he could, like he was trying to connect with a fastball, and slammed the hooked point of the poker against Tom Dockin's knee.

He'd expected to hear a bone break, or at least the flesh to sizzle when the cold iron struck it, but Tom Dockin just looked at him and said, "Ow" in a toneless voice. The giant knelt, and Gabriel climbed up on his back, settling onto his shoulders.

"Did you think iron would hurt my Tom?" Gabriel said. "His *teeth* are made of iron. He's a giant, not a fairy. It's an important distinction. Your little metal stick will be useful for swatting flower fairies out of the sky, I'd wager. Go enjoy yourself while you can, Ryan. I suggest you return to your world. You'll be living in fairyland soon enough."

"I'll stop you," Ryan said. "And I'll stop Herne too."

"May as well try to drink the ocean, boy," Gabriel said, almost kindly. "Herne is more than you can handle. And please don't try—I'd hate for you to get yourself killed and spoil my plan to escape." He tugged Tom Dockin's ears, and the giant stomped away.

Ryan sat down in the leaves with the fireplace poker across his knees. Just a piece of metal, not even any good against giants, but better than nothing. He'd have preferred an Enchanted Sword of Skull-Cleaving or a Sentient Blade of Flying Razors, but you made do with what you got.

There had to be a way to beat Herne—or at least convince him to set Silas free and keep Gabriel trapped here. He tried to think of a plan, but he didn't come up with much, so he started walking. Wandering by himself in the Deep Woods of fairyland probably wasn't the best idea, but he wasn't accomplishing much sitting on his butt. When in doubt, *do something*—that's what his mom always said.

He walked along a little deer path, which eventually led to a still pool surrounded by eight or nine trees, their branches extending out over the water. Ryan looked around for teenage girls armed with rocks or other perils, but the place was deserted. He went to a smooth, mossy rock at the edge of the nearly circular pool and sat down, staring at his reflection in the dark water.

Ryan *liked* his face. He didn't want Gabriel Ratchet wearing it.

The water rippled and a silvery fish poked its head out of the water. "Hello, Ryan," it said. "I'm the salmon of wisdom."

"I feel like I should jump up and shout or something," Ryan said, "but honestly, a talking fish is not the weirdest thing I've seen today. So you're the salmon of wisdom—does that mean you're going to tell me how 'early to bed, early to rise, makes a man healthy and wealthy and wise,' like Puck did when he got wisdom?"

"Not at all," the salmon said. "I like to sleep late, myself."

"There's a magical salmon in the game," Ryan remembered. "It lives in a pool way up in the mountains, in a place you can't even get to unless your character can fly—and I'm way too low level to fly. Dad spent about a week trying to fish for that salmon and never got him. If you catch him and eat him, it increases all your stats—intelligence, charisma, strength, fortitude, everything—by three points permanently."

"Doesn't quite have the poetry I'd like," the salmon said, "but I guess it's not a bad way to be remembered. I'm here to help you, Ryan."

"Great. Here to send me on another quest?" Nuts from the trees were scattered all over the ground, and Ryan picked one up and tossed it into the water. The salmon dove after it, swallowed it whole, and then emerged again in the same spot as before.

"Something like that," the salmon said. "I've been waiting to talk to you when Silas wasn't around. If I tried to explain the true nature of this place to him, he wouldn't believe me. But you might."

Ryan leaned forward. "True nature? What do you mean?"

"This isn't fairyland," the salmon said. "As far as I know, there's no such thing as fairies."

"That's ridiculous. I saw tree branches wearing suits. People with the faces of cats. Tom Dockin, and Herne the hunter!"

"True," the salmon said, "but those are all illusions. Sure, they can kill you and eat you, but that doesn't mean they're exactly real. This whole place is nothing but a glamour, and Silas is the one casting it. He grew up hearing stories about Jenny Greenteeth and Tom Dockin and Herne and the fields beyond the fields, so that's what he sees here. His imagination created all of this—fairyland and everyone in it—and he doesn't even realize it. The reason Silas can't escape fairyland is because he believes it's *impossible* to escape fairyland. That's why your quest failed—deep down, Silas believed it *had* to fail."

"You're saying... Silas has, like, magical powers?"

The salmon shook its head, which was a really weird thing to see. "Not at all. You have just as much power to change things as Silas does, potentially... It's just that he's been here a lot longer, and his vision is more deeply ingrained. Difficult to overcome. But little flashes of *your* imagination come through too—the Trow King, and the goblin market, and even your glimpse of Herne in his iron armor. You conjured all of that into existence."

"So Silas and I are... both wizards?" Ryan squinted at the salmon and wished it would turn into a sea lion, but nothing happened.

"No, no. Anyone could do it. Any person could change this world, though it seems to work better with children, perhaps because their imaginations are wilder or because they're more willing to believe. Listen," the salmon said. "There's something that lives in these woods. It's been here for a long time. It's alive, sort of. And it's very stupid—beyond stupid. Literally mindless. But it has power—the power to shape reality. And when a human being with an imagination encounters it, the creature looks into that person's mind, down deep, and starts to change reality, and create a world. Not necessarily a nice world, but a new world. And if the person imagines scary things, the creature becomes scary. This creature has tried to show itself to Silas a few times, but Silas's imagination just makes it part of this world, into another fairy monster.

He calls it the Boneless, or the It. But really, the Boneless is the only magic in this place."

"The Boneless. Okay, if you say so. What does it want?"

"It wants to be *free*," the salmon said. "Silas encountered it in the wood long ago, and knew right away it was magic—or at least unnatural—and assumed it was a fairy creature. From that first thought, this whole world sprang. Silas believes he's trapped in fairyland . . . but that means the Boneless is trapped too, because you can't have a jail without a warden. That's why it . . . why we . . . why *I* was so happy to see you. You came to Silas with a new vision for how fairyland could work: you could do a quest, and you could escape. I thought you would succeed . . . but then, at the last minute, Silas's doubt was too great, and he turned the whole quest into a cruel joke by Herne."

"This barely makes any sense to me," Ryan said. "What am I supposed to do exactly?"

"Convince Silas that you can set him free," the salmon said. "Convince him that you can defeat Herne. He believes Herne is the master of this place, and if you beat Herne, Silas will finally allow himself to leave fairyland."

"But what happens to the Boneless if Silas leaves?" Ryan said. "If it doesn't have a mind of its own, if it needs a human imagination to give it a shape, won't it go back to being a blob of nothing once Silas is gone?"

"Oh, don't worry about us," the salmon said. "We'll be fine. We don't mind being mindless."

"What do you mean you'll be . . . oh. You're the Boneless."

"I'm the salmon of wisdom," the salmon said, "but I'm an aspect of the Boneless, just like Herne and Tom Dockin and Beag's daughters and the Trow King and Ghillie Dhu. All created by the Boneless, with help from your imagination or Silas's."

"And Gabriel's, right?" Ryan said.

The salmon opened and closed its mouth a few times. "Gabriel. Yes. Of course. Though, ah, he doesn't have as much imagination as he used to, you know—that's why I forgot him."

"But if Silas knew all this, if I told him, I'm sure he'd just *leave*. Why not tell him?"

"We've tried, but he doesn't believe it. He thinks it's a fairy trick."

"Um," Ryan said. "How do I know it's not a fairy trick?"

"I'm the salmon of wisdom. I don't play tricks. I impart great secret truths."

"Does Gabriel know?"

"Absolutely not. Can you imagine how viciously he'd exploit the fact if he *did* know? The kind of changes he could make? Better that one stays ignorant. Defeat Herne, and Gabriel will go free too, so it won't matter. In fact, you should get Gabriel to help you in the fight."

Ryan stood up. "Ha! Right. Why would I even try to do that?"

"Like your mother said, you need a good group to beat Herne the hunter," the salmon said. "And Gabriel's magic is powerful. He has a giant following his orders too, and that can't hurt."

"I can't believe I'm taking advice from a fish," Ryan said. "Where can I find Silas?"

The salmon sighed, which was even weirder than seeing a salmon shake its head. "He thought he would be punished for trying to escape, so, of course, he *has* been. Dragged into the barrowlands and forced to serve at one of their horrible parties."

"Why do that to him?" Ryan said. "It's just cruel."

"Because Silas expects it. The Boneless really has very little control—we are what Silas makes us. We can only talk to you like this because your imagination allows for the possibility of magical beings providing exposition to help you understand quests, because of that game you play—and we can only talk to you now because Silas isn't around, overriding your imagination with his own. But the longer you're here, the stronger you get, and the more your mind will influence this place."

"I'm trying to imagine a flying horse to ride," Ryan said, "and nothing's happening."

"Wrong mythology," the salmon said. "Wouldn't be compatible with the prevailing conditions. And anyway, you can't really do things like that consciously—the Boneless draws images from deep inside your mind, and controlling it is harder than controlling your own dreams. I'm afraid you can't just wish superpowers for yourself."

"Naturally," Ryan said. "That would make things too easy."

"It's your own fault," the salmon said. "Deep down, you think quests should be hard if they're really important. Go save Silas, and defeat Herne, and get us *all* out of these woods." The salmon vanished under the water.

10

R YAN DIDN'T REMEMBER EXACTLY HOW TO GET BACK TO the barrowlands, so he just started walking. If the shape of this place really was based entirely on imagination, then maybe just trying to reach the barrowlands would be enough to get him there. At least he had his fireplace poker, though it was heavy lugging it around. Still, based on the way Silas's single nail had stopped an army of barrowland revelers in their tracks, the iron would come in handy. He would have preferred having a few of those superpowers he couldn't just wish for though . . .

He looked up, realizing he'd been lost in thought for a while, fantasizing about super strength, invisibility, the ability to fly fast as lightning. The trees had thinned out, and the sky had gone all gray and cloudy, and the landscape was much rockier and more sharp, like he'd somehow wandered into the mountains . . . though his legs would probably hurt a lot worse if he'd really just walked up a mountainside. Ryan looked around, hoping for something familiar . . . and saw a half-collapsed castle clinging to the rocks some miles away. "Oh, no way," he murmured. This view was *exactly* like one of the computer desktop wallpapers you could download off the *Wild Hunt Online* website, and the castle was the home of the snake lady Melusine, final boss of one of the hardest dungeons in the game. No way *this* was part of Silas's vision of fairyland; this was pure Ryan, all the way.

He wasn't about to step into that castle. You couldn't fight a bunch of wights and snake people with a fireplace poker, even if it was cold iron. Which, his mother said, was really just a fancy old-fashioned way of saying "iron"—even steel was deadly to fairies in the old stories, though some people nowadays said that "cold iron" meant iron that had never been forged with fire. The game never really explained what it meant, but Ryan thought the fire poker counted . . . which meant it *would* count. But even Ryan's character, who had a magical bow and enchanted leather armor, wouldn't dare enter Melusine's castle, not for another couple dozen levels, and even then, only with a good group.

But there was something else special about this location. There was a peddler who walked up and down this path. Ryan had never been able to buy anything from him, because he appeared only once a day, at random times, and high-level characters waited for him all day and all night and fought for the chance to be the first to reach him. Every day, that peddler sold a single mystery item, and it was different every time. You had to buy the item sight unseen, and the price was the same for everybody:

It cost all the money you had.

Aengus took all your character's hard-earned money, whether you had a single copper piece or a thousand platinum. You had to have at least one copper, though—Aengus wouldn't give you something for nothing. Nine times out of ten, the item he sold you turned out to be something pretty good—magical gloves that let you swing a sword faster than the eye could follow, or a staff that could magically wrap your enemies in vines, or a hammer that caused little earthquakes. You could either use what you bought or sell it to recoup some of the money you'd lost.

But about 10 percent of the time, the peddler sold you something incredibly rare: A key that could open any locked door in the game. A small diamond that was as big as a house inside, where you could rest safely and recover your health without having to pay an innkeeper. A whistle that summoned one of the game's ghostly black dogs and let you keep it as a pet—his mom had gotten that one, actually, and jokingly named the monstrous mount Gert, after their black lab. And sometimes the peddler sold even rarer things, unique items that only one person at a time in the whole game world could own.

Ryan sat down on a rock and squinted along the crooked, stony path. After a while an old man, bent almost double by the weight of his pack, with a white beard down to his knees, approached, hobbling along with a walking stick in each hand. When he got close enough, Ryan said, "Hello, Wandering Aengus. What do you have to sell today?"

"Same thing I have to sell every day." Aengus eased himself down on the rock next to Ryan. "The pack on my back. And what's in it, well—who can say?"

"And what would it cost me to buy that pack?"

Aengus shrugged. "Whatever's jingling in your pockets, my son."

"You seem like a pretty old guy, though," Ryan said. "What if I just took it?"

Aengus grinned, though there weren't many teeth involved. "You can try." It was, in fact, technically possible to defeat Wandering Aengus in battle. His dad's guild had done it once. It took twenty high-level characters the best part of half an hour to kill him, incurring heavy losses along the way, and when the last man standing tore the pack off Aengus's back, there was nothing inside but a wedge of moldy cheese that made your character sick if they ate it.

"That's okay," Ryan said. He fished the coin Silas had given him out of his pocket. Giving it up would mean he couldn't go back to his world and return to fairyland . . . But that was all right. He wasn't going to be leaving anytime soon, and when he did, he sincerely hoped there wouldn't be a fairyland left to come back to. "This is all I have."

Aengus sighed. "Big spender. Listen, before we complete our transaction, I want to give you a piece of friendly advice. Don't listen to everything that smart aleck fish has to say."

"The salmon of wisdom? What do you mean?"

"You asked a good question back there." Aengus stared up at the jagged outline of Melusine's castle. "What *does* happen to the Boneless if Silas and you leave? The salmon said not to worry about it. But maybe . . . maybe you should worry about it. The Boneless is alive, sort of. At least, it's alive enough that it needs to eat, and what it eats is imagination. The Boneless *feeds* on your imaginings. Now, I say it feeds, but it doesn't really take anything from you—no more than you take heat away from a fire when you warm yourself beside it; the fire would have shed that heat anyway, and it can always generate more. Humans and their imaginings are the same way: fires, giving off heat. But the Boneless *does* need people, and their minds, to sustain itself."

"So it's like one of those horror movie things that feeds on fear," Ryan said. "Appearing to little kids looking like a monster in the closet or a clown with a big knife, freaking them out and eating their emotions. Right?"

"Sort of," Aengus said. "It doesn't have to be fear. You're not especially afraid now, and the Boneless is *feasting* on you. The Boneless can feed on wonderful happy imaginings too . . . but this fairyland is mostly Silas's place, and his imagination has made it a dark place. Fear is just as good as joy, as far as the Boneless is concerned. It doesn't care what you imagine, as long as you imagine it vividly."

"But . . . you must be part of the Boneless too. So why are you telling me something different from what the salmon told me?"

He shrugged. "Don't ask me. You shape this place. Maybe because I'm entirely born from your imagination, while the salmon was mostly from Silas's mind. Your friend expects fairyland to be a treacherous place full of liars, and so the salmon told you lies. But remember: the Boneless is always hungry. If it wants Silas to leave the forest, maybe it's because the Boneless is tired of just having one mind to feed on, and wants to feast on the billions of minds in the wider world."

"It's got two minds to feed on, though," Ryan said. "Gabriel's mind too. Right?"

Aengus nodded. "Right. Sorry. I'm getting old. And Gabriel's imagination isn't all it used to be."

The salmon had forgotten Gabriel too. Weird. Ryan had that feeling again, that he was right on the edge of figuring out something important.

Then Aengus took the coin from Ryan's hand and dropped his pack at Ryan's feet. "Enjoy. I hope it helps." He strode off down the path, no longer bent over, spinning a walking stick in each hand like a baton twirler in a parade. When he was over the hill and out of sight, Ryan reached down and touched the straps on the pack.

Please be a magic sword, he thought. A magic sword would be *so cool*, infinitely more awesome than the length of gray, ash-stained fireplace poker he currently had for a weapon.

But when he opened the pack, there wasn't a sword. Instead, there was something much better: a curling ram's horn, the color of old piano keys, with a long leather strap attached. A slip of paper was curled up into a tube and tucked inside the mouthpiece, and when Ryan unrolled it, the paper read, "Herne's Second-Best Horn."

"Holy shut-your-mouth," Ryan said. This was one of the rarest of the rare, a unique drop, and one of the single most powerful items in the game. Once a day, you could blow the horn and summon the Wild Hunt, which would spend ten minutes protecting you and attacking any of your enemies. This wasn't the cutesy half-sized Wild Hunt you could summon by wearing Herne's Second-Best Helm, which quite a few players had, but the serious, full-sized, almost unstoppable horde of hounds and elven hunters that randomly ravaged the Endless Forest. This horn was the next best thing to a Win This Battle Free card, as there were literally only four or five enemies in the game that could stand against the onslaught of the Wild Hunt—and even the Triple Witch or Melusine or Herne himself would take a serious beating in the process. The cool thing was, the Hunt would sweep up any other enemies or monsters it happened to pass by, and make them fight for you too. And Ryan had the horn that called them. For *real* (or close enough to real).

Whatever was going to happen would happen today, though, so he'd only get one chance to use the horn. Which meant he'd have to choose his moment wisely.

Ryan tossed the empty pack aside and slung the horn over his shoulder. He wasn't even worried about someone—not even Gabriel Ratchet—stealing it; the horn was a soul-linked item, which meant it wouldn't work for anyone but the owner. You couldn't even *give* soul-linked magical items away.

Iron in my hand and horn over my shoulder, he thought. *I'm coming for you, Herne.*

But first, he had to free Silas.

The twisting mountain path wound down the far side of the hill, leaving Melusine's castle looming behind him. Was there anyone in the castle now, he wondered? Or would it remain empty unless he walked up and banged his poker on the portcullis, waiting for his mind to fill it with snake-bodied women and the ghosts of dead adventurers?

Eventually the path leveled out, and the sky took on the pale cast he remembered from his morning visit to the barrowlands. The sun looked like a nickel found on the floorboard of a car, its shininess covered in a layer of grime. He walked toward the long barrow and found the same door in the side as before. The nail was gone, though he could still see the hole where Silas had hammered it in with his shoe—only this morning? It seemed so long ago, but then, time could be funny in fairyland. Not so different from the game—you sat down to play, and it seemed like only a few minutes had passed before your mom or dad said, "Okay, your hour's up! Go read a book or build a better mousetrap or something!" When you were immersed in doing something you cared about, time had a way of disappearing out from under you in a very pleasant way.

Ryan pushed open the door, wincing at the creak of hinges, and poked his head inside.

The ballroom was there, same as before, but most of the candles in the chandeliers were out, and the long tables were bare of food, and there were no dancers or waiters or musicians . . . but also no guards.

Scratch that. When Ryan stepped in and closed the door behind him, he noticed the egg-shaped man sprawled in an armchair beside the door with an axe the size of a snow shovel resting across his legs. He snored gently and muttered to himself, thin lips smacking.

As far as guards went, he wasn't very terrifying, so Ryan crept in to the ballroom—and saw, at the far end, hunched on either side of a card table, Silas and the Trow King. He hurried to them, glancing back to make sure the egg man was still asleep. "Silas!" he whisper-called. "Let's get out of here!"

Silas just shook his head and looked back down at the table—where, it appeared, he was playing a game with the Trow King. The game didn't make much sense to Ryan, because Silas was playing with chess pieces, while the Trow King had checkers. Silas moved a bishop, and the Trow King jumped over it with a checker and chortled. "I should have seen that coming," Silas said. He beckoned to Ryan and pointed to an empty wooden chair off to one side. "Join us. This game is even more enjoyable when played by three people."

"You're playing games?" Ryan moved the chair over as quietly as he could, though maybe being discreet wasn't necessary, since neither Silas nor the Trow King seemed to be trying to keep quiet. "I expected you to be . . . I don't know. Having something horrible happen to you. I thought I was going to have to break you out of jail."

"This is a jail, of a sort," Silas said, pushing a pawn forward one space, "though the punishment is less than I'd expected, thanks to our friend."

The Trow King hopped a checker to the far side of Silas's board and yelled, "King me!" in a voice so booming it made his sausage nose wobble. The egg man by the door didn't react at all, just snored a little louder. "Ha," the Trow King said. "King the king!"

Silas balanced a pawn on top of the Trow King's checker and sighed. "Originally, Herne ordered that I should be beaten with a switch of brambles and made to clean out the pens of the fairy deer—which create quite large quantities of manure for creatures so small. But the Trow King convinced our keeper"—Silas inclined his head toward the egg man—"that a far crueler punishment would be forcing me to keep the Trow King himself company."

"He hates me," the Trow King said. "All of them do. Because I like fistfights better than duels, trampolines better than curtsies, and whooping better than whispering. They think I'm the most uncouth unbearable unspeakable unpleasant fellow ever to set foot in fairyland, and what punishment could be worse than being forced to spend time with *me*?"

"Being beaten with brambles, for one," Silas said, "and cleaning up manure, for another. But I said, 'Oh, no, not that, anything but that, nothing could be more dreadful,' so here I am. I never would have expected a trick like that to work, but the Trow King said to trust him, so I did."

I am changing things, Ryan thought. The Trow King came from *his* imagination, and he'd helped save Silas from his own dark expectations. "I'm glad they're not making things too terrible for you, but Silas—we can still get you out of here."

"The creature by the door seems to be sleeping," Silas said, "and perhaps he is. But if I try to leave, he will wake. He doesn't care who enters this barrow . . . but he cares very much who leaves."

"Okay, that's a problem we'll have to deal with," Ryan said. "But I didn't mean we can get you out of just this room—I meant we can get you out of *fairyland*. We can defeat Herne."

"Impossible," Silas said. "Confront him directly? We could not prevail."

"I tried and failed," the Trow King said.

Ryan winced. *Whose side are you on, anyway?* "I don't think it's impossible," Ryan said. "Not now that I have this." He put the horn down on the table, next to a cluster of captured checkers and chessmen.

Silas prodded it with his finger. "Looks like a ram's horn. Makes a dreadful noise if you blow on it, I'm sure, but not a clamor loud enough to drive away Herne."

"No," the Trow King said, croaking with awe. "That's one of *Herne's own* horns, isn't it?"

"His second best," Ryan said. "I bought it off an old man wandering in the mountains."

"What mountains?" Silas said, but the Trow King just nodded sagely.

"Ah, yes, the Wandering Aengus," he said. "I've always wondered how he got such wonderful items to sell. With this . . . my boy, you might have a chance. But even with the horn, you'd need a fearsome bunch of allies to make it to the heart of Herne's wood."

"Well, I thought we'd have me and Silas and, if you're willing, Trow King, *you*."

"Ah, well, there's some trouble there." The Trow King looked away. "I'm bound here, by the word of this barrow's lord, Master Ovo." He nodded toward the egg man by the door. "I made the mistake of eating his food, and now I'm bound until he chooses to release me. Which I don't think he'll do, as Herne has ordered him to keep me here."

Footsteps sounded from the shadows at the far end of the room. Gabriel Ratched strolled toward them, chewing on an apple. "Then we'll just have to scare him more than Herne does," he said.

11

"CHESSMATE IN FOUR MOVES, TROW KING," GABRIEL SAID, leaning past Ryan to peer at the board. "Do you see it?"

"Who's the dirty human boy?" the Trow King said. "Friend of yours?"

"Not a friend." Silas crossed his arms over his chest. "Someone I have feared, though less so in your company." Ryan was proud to see Silas standing up to Gabriel, instead of sucking up to him.

"Yeah, he's pretty much an enemy," Ryan said, gripping his fireplace poker. Gabriel, being human, wouldn't be magically vulnerable to iron . . . but he'd be *normally* vulnerable to iron, and being hit with a poker would feel lousy for anybody.

"I'm crushed," Gabriel said. "I've been following Ryan around, just waiting for a chance to offer my services, and when I step forward, I'm insulted?"

"Oh," Ryan said. "You heard I had one of Herne's horns, so now you want in on *our* plan."

Gabriel shrugged. "Overthrowing Herne seems like more fun than *my* plan, which would, after all, require me to live in Ryan's dull little life. But I'd still trade the lot of you in for a gross of cats so I could cast the Taghairm spell instead. So what's the immediate issue? We need to gather a powerful group to take on Herne, right? Obviously I would be an asset to such a group."

"I do not trust him, Ryan," Silas said. "He lies as easily as you and I breathe."

"Not quite that easily," Gabriel said. "Say, as easily as you fart, maybe. But my magical studies tell me I can't blow the horn—only Ryan can—and I can't breach Herne's wood without assistance. The Trow King is a formidable fighter. I have magic. Tom Dockin is our muscle. And Silas, even I must admit, is an exceedingly agile, tireless, and stealthy for a useless brat. As a team, I think we have a chance."

"What do you think, Silas? Do you want to try to take down Herne, or . . . just play checkers?"

"It's called chessers," the Trow King said helpfully.

Silas closed his eyes for a moment, then opened them, and finally smiled. "All right. Before today, I thought that escaping from this realm was impossible. And the failure of our quest this morning only made me more sure. But in all great stories, there is a time of despair that must be overcome in order to eventually triumph. I will try again, Ryan, and hope this new story will be a happier one."

"I always like stories where heroes and villains have to team up to fight a common enemy," Gabriel said. "Don't you?"

"I think most of the really interesting bad guys in stories don't *think* they're bad guys," Ryan said. "They're just doing what they think they have to do."

"Not me," Gabriel said. "I do what I *want* to do. Villains always get the best lines, and the best costumes, anyway. I'm happy to be a villain . . . but Herne's a bigger villain than me, so he's got to go. Shall we go storm the castle?"

"We should take Puck too," Ryan said.

Gabriel rolled his eyes. "Why? What good is he in his current condition?"

"He's done more for us than you ever have, Gabe," Ryan said.

"Don't call me Gabe, *Rye*."

"We will take Puck," Silas said, standing. "He is locked in a cupboard. The master of this barrow has the key."

"Fine. We'll make Humpty Dumpty give us the key when we force him to set King Ugly free." Gabriel held out his hand. "Give me the fireplace poker. You don't know how long I've wished I could have an iron bar over here."

Ryan hesitated. "What are you going to do? You won't . . . "

"Kill him? No, he can't set the Trow King free if he's dead, and anyway, fairies are tough to kill, even with a nice length of iron. But they can be hurt, and wounds inflicted by iron don't heal. Ever have a broken bone, *Rye*? Can you imagine having a broken arm for the rest of your life, and the rest of your life lasts *forever*? I'll just threaten him. He'll give in."

Ryan offered Gabriel the poker. Gabriel took it, and started to swing it at Ryan's head, stopping short. Ryan, who didn't even flinch, just stared at him. "You're no fun anymore since you got that horn," Gabriel said.

"You need me," Ryan said, "a lot more than I need you. I won't tell you to be nice, because I don't think you know how, but you don't scare me."

"Feh," Gabriel said, and walked across the room toward the egg man, swinging the poker in vicious little arcs through the air. He walked to the door of the barrow, and Ryan thought he planned to take off, stealing the poker, but instead he just tugged the door open and then turned toward Master Ovo, hiding the weapon behind his back.

The egg man sprang to his stubby feet. "You, boy—no one leaves this barrow without my permission."

"Then I'm asking your permission. And not just for me—for everyone currently inside."

Master Ovo shook his head, except he didn't have a head, so he just sort of rotated his whole enormous body back and forth a few times. "You're in my house now, child. And there you will remain." He leaned forward, squinting. "I know you. What was your name? Galadriel Rampant? No, that's more of a girl's name. Globulous Ransack? You have some little scraps of fairy magic. Would you be foolish enough to try your magic on me, a master of magic, little Globulous?"

"It's Gabriel," Gabriel said, whipping the poker around and pointing it at the egg man. "Ratchet. And you are Master Ovo. The egg lord. Someday you're supposed to hatch into something truly amazing, aren't you? A bird with wings of fire, wasn't it? Or was it some sort of enormous lizard? I haven't read my latest copy of *Who's Who in Fairyland Society*, so the details are a little fuzzy." He advanced on Master Ovo, who stepped back, his tiny eyes fixed on the iron weapon. Gabriel kept coming until Ovo was backed up against a wall, then gently pressed the end of the weapon against the egg man's vast, white, shelled belly. "But you'll never get a chance to hatch if I poke a hole in you and let your yolk run out. You'll just be a shell of a man. A shell! Of a man! Puck would say, 'Ho, ho, ho,' at this point, don't you think?"

"I'm not afraid of a boy with a stick," Ovo said, though he sounded extremely afraid.

"Pressure is an interesting thing." Gabriel pushed the poker forward, just a bit. Ovo grunted, and there was a tiny *crack*. "There. Normally your shell is hard as stone, I know, but remember, I'm holding iron ... and your magic doesn't work on iron. I applied just enough pressure to crack your outer shell, but not quite enough to pierce the shell membrane inside, the bubble of skin that holds in all your insides. Of course, if I applied a little more pressure, all your insides would start running out, and if I pushed a bit harder still, I could break your yolk. It would all be rather messy, but you'd cease to be a problem for me."

"You won't kill me," Ovo said. "If I die, your friends Silas and the Trow King will be trapped here. They accepted my hospitality, though I admit we had to force a cup of water down the boy's throat—they can't depart without my permission."

"True. Which is why, instead, I'm going to continue to apply just a little pressure ... first here." Gabriel pushed in another spot, and there was another little crack. "And then here." *Crack.* "And then *here.*" *Crack.* "Until you're nothing but a spiderwebbed mass of fissures. Then I'll gently, gently flick off bits of shell until you're nothing but a paper-thin membrane in a waistcoat ... and the first time you get a splinter or annoy a cat enough that it scratches you, that will be the end of you. How does that sound?" *Crack.* "You can stop this at any time. Just free my friends and give us the key to the cupboard where you keep Puck."

Crack.

"All right!" Master Ovo shouted. "I give my permission, and set the human boy Silas and the Trow King free!" He fumbled in a vest pocket—his stubby arms made it difficult—and tossed a key on the floor. "There! I did as you wished!"

"Much appreciated," Gabriel said. "But I think I'll break you anyway. You can't make an omelet ... " He reared back his arm, raising the poker high ...

And the Trow King plucked it from his hands and threw it aside, hissing in pain from his brief contact with the iron. Ryan snatched up the weapon and handed it to Silas, who accepted it solemnly.

Gabriel sighed. "You people. He has magic, you know. He could cause trouble for us later. Killing him is the only way to be—"

"Swear an oath that you will remain here until the sun sets and rises again," Silas said, pointing the poker toward Master Ovo. "And make contact with no one."

"I so swear!" Master Ovo gasped.

"Repeat the words," Silas said, and the egg man did so.

"Fairies keep their oaths." Silas lowered the weapon. "They go to great lengths to avoid making oaths, and will twist their words mightily to create advantages for themselves, but when they make a promise, they are compelled to keep it. Killing is not the only way, Gabriel Ratchet."

"Yes, fine. It's just the most entertaining way. Believe me, I'd know—I've entertained myself that way a lot over the years. Here's the key. Let's go open the cupboard and welcome the most useless member of our merry band."

Master Ovo sank back into his armchair, delicately touching his many cracked places. "Smear a bit of clay on the cracks," the Trow King said. "And heat them. They'll form a new shell."

"Thank you, savage," Master Ovo said. "But my physicians need not resort to such primitive methods, I'm sure."

The Trow King shrugged and turned back to his companions. "The cupboard where they locked Puck is over here." He shook his head. "I can't believe all that time I drank from him, I never knew the cup was Puck. It explains the foul taste though." He led the way back toward his corner of the ballroom and pointed to a tall wooden cabinet mounted on the wall. Gabriel fitted the key into the lock, twisted it, and the doors burst open.

A man just slightly taller than Gabriel tumbled out, thumping to the floor with a groan. He was dressed all in green and had pointed ears and mossy hair. "That cupboard was a terribly tight fit. Odd, as it seemed quite roomy when I was a cup."

"Puck!" Ryan said. "You got your powers back!"

"If only." He sat up, rubbing the side of his head. "The Horned Lord just thought it would be amusing to give me one of my old favorite forms back, only to stuff me in a cabinet. 'Ho, ho, ho,' he said. Sounded ridiculous. The intonation was all wrong."

"So he's still useless," Gabriel said, "but at least now he can walk. That's something, anyway. I don't suppose there's anything useful in the cabinet? A magic sword, perhaps? Several dozen cats?"

"Alas, no," Puck said. "Or, in the case of the cats: fortunately, no. Nothing in there but an old silver spoon and a wooded ladle and a broken shoe and a tin whistle."

Ryan looked into the cupboard. He couldn't be sure, but . . . well, whistles were useful in the game. Usually. Unless they were cursed. He pocketed the whistle and turned back to his friends.

Gabriel made a great show of sighing. "Then we continue with plan . . . What plan is this? Plan D? I've lost track of my own plots. It happens when you have as many good ideas as I do."

"Puck," Ryan said, "we're going to fight Herne. Will you help us?"

"Help a snowball attack the sun? Certainly. Why not?"

"They have one of Herne's horns," the Trow King rumbled.

"Ah," Puck said, rising to his feet. "That changes things. Our pack could cancel out *his* pack, which means we'd just have to face the Horned Lord himself, and, let's see, we're one, two, three, four, five against one . . . Still terrible odds, but not *hopeless* ones. If only Silas and Ryan had some magic . . . Ah, well. What you lack in magic you make up for in perseverance and pluck, and those have taken us this far."

"Yes. As far as this barrow, where we started," Gabriel said. "And anyway, we're six—Tom Dockin will join us. He's good at hitting things."

"Ah, good," Puck said. "I bring so many brains to the group, it's good to balance that with some additional brawn."

"We should go," Ryan said. "The borders between this place and my world are only open for today, and I don't want to be trapped here." He started for the door, because any group of people with places to go will stand around talking forever unless one of them actually sets an example and starts moving.

Silas fell into step beside him. "I agree setting Puck free was the right thing do to," he said, "but remember, he is a tricksy fairy, and not to be trusted. He helped us once, but that does not necessarily mean he can be relied on for all times in the future."

Oh, great. Now Puck might betray us, Ryan thought. *I wish Silas could learn to trust people.* "Puck has as much reason as you do to hate Herne," Ryan said. "The guy made him be a cup for years."

"That is true," Silas said, and Ryan hoped it would be enough.

As they passed by Master Ovo, the egg man called out, "Clay, you say?"

The Trow King paused. "Try the banks of the White River. Good clay there, and it will even match the color of your shell." They filed through the doorway, and Tom Dockin was there, taller than the Trow King, even crouching with his tennis racket–sized hands resting on his knees. The giant rose up. "I don't know how you stand it in a place so small and tight. Tom Dockin can't abide small spaces."

"Your little psychological quirks are endlessly fascinating to us," Gabriel said. "Bend down. I'm tired of all this walking."

"We fight now?" Tom said, lifting Gabriel up to his shoulders. "I eat these children?"

"Later. First we have to go overthrow the Horned Lord . . . "

Tom Dockin shook himself like a wet dog, and Gabriel flew from his shoulders with a squawk, crashing to the ground. "Our bargain is broken," Tom said. "Goodbye, Gabriel Ratchet. I will eat you someday." The giant turned away.

"Wait! We had a binding agreement! You can't leave, you're my slave!"

"I made an oath to you," Tom said, "but I have an older oath to the Horned Lord. I can do him no harm. When obeying one oath means breaking another, the oldest oath takes precedence. It is a basic rule of our laws—but a child like you would not know that." Tom Dockin stomped away.

"I do not think I have ever seen Gabriel Ratchet make such a mistake before," Silas said. "He usually plans things a dozen moves ahead, like life is a game of chessers."

"He's just a kid," Ryan said. "Not a supervillain. And he's barely even a kid anymore, if he's traded away so many of his memories. But he's smart, and he still has magic, so I guess we'll keep him."

"We don't need that giant anyway." Gabriel dusted himself off and limped over to join the group. "Dumb brute. And with the Trow King, we've got our dumb brute quota filled already."

"Do we truly need this boy?" the Trow King said. "I could throw him into the sky. I might even hit the moon."

"Just try to touch me, savage—"

"Enough!" Ryan shouted. "First we fight Herne. Then, if you really want, we can fight ourselves. But the Horned Lord first. We have to find his wood."

"I know the way," Silas said. "It is long, and perilous, and filled with dangers. I think it likely we will not all survive. We must begin by entering the caves of Sawney Bean, where the inhuman descendants of the legendary cannibal—"

"No, no, it's okay. I know a shortcut," Ryan said. "Uh, it'll still be dangerous, of course"—It *had* to be dangerous, Silas wouldn't believe they could get to Herne without going someplace dangerous first—"but not nearly so long."

"This is a path you discovered in your . . . puppet theater game?" Silas said.

"Yep. We just need to find a mushroom ring."

"I know of one," Puck said. "I'll lead the way. Look at how much I'm contributing already. Where would you be without me?" He set off for the woods, and the others fell in behind him.

Ryan was afraid Silas would ask him more details about the shortcut, but it seemed Silas trusted him, at least—that was something. Ryan just hoped his plan would work . . . which meant he needed to *believe* it would work. The game world of the Endless Forest was—while not literally infinite—very, very large. Getting from place to place without having to walk through monster-infested forest every step of the way was an important part of the game. So there were magical animals you could ride, boats that would whisk you along interconnected waterways, and other methods of fast travel, including the mushroom rings and the standing stones. Circles of fungus and rings of tall stones appeared all over the Endless Forest, and they were interconnected. Stepping into one ring allowed you to step *out* of any other ring. The only problem was, the rings tended to be defended. If you were high enough level to use a given ring, the guards let you by without any trouble. If you were low level, though, you had to fight for the right to travel instantaneously—and, being low level, the odds were you'd die, unless you had powerful friends to help you beat the guards.

Ryan was willing to bet his group could best pretty much any guard the Endless Forest could throw at them . . . assuming that they all worked together.

And that Gabriel didn't turn on them.

And that Silas's imagination didn't make matters any worse.

12

Puck led them through the Deep Woods to a clearing filled with white-capped, red-spotted mushrooms. In the game, mushroom rings were a dozen or so fungi arrayed in a circle, but this was different: a space utterly filled with hundreds of mushrooms, except for a perfectly round place in the middle about ten feet in diameter. The space inside the circle was bare black dirt, without even a single fallen leaf or broken twig. In *WHO*, fairy rings looked whimsical and magical; this just looked like a place where the earth itself was somehow poisoned and blighted. Once, Ryan's family had taken a road trip and stopped to see a famous place about two hours west of home, called the Devil's Tramping Ground. The spot was a circle—forty feet across—in the middle of the woods, where nothing had grown for more than a hundred years. According to legend, the Devil himself liked to pace in a circle there, thinking up new ways to torment mankind, and as far as Ryan knew, nobody had come up with a better explanation for the barren track. This circle in the mushrooms reminded him uncomfortably of that place.

Gabriel Ratchet strode forward, kicking mushrooms aside—they puffed out clouds of spores around his ankles—and clearing a path to the ring. "This is our express elevator to Herne's wood?"

"Yes." Ryan sounded more confident than he truly felt. "We'll step into the ring, and it will transport us to a circle of standing stones near Herne's lair."

Gabriel stepped inside the ring and crossed his arms. "Come on then."

The Trow King went in, followed by Puck, and Silas and Ryan came last. "I fear what we might find waiting for us on the other side," Silas said.

"I really wish you wouldn't do that," Ryan said. "Don't borrow trouble, okay?"

"I believe in being hopeful," Silas replied, "but also in being prepared."

They entered the ring, and stood around eyeing one another and the mushrooms. "Are we supposed to join hands or something?" Gabriel said. "Maybe do a little chant?"

In the game, when you stepped into a circle, a little menu popped up on screen listing all the possible destinations. Names in green were places you could go fairly safely. Names in yellow were dangerous but survivable. Names in red were instant death. There was no such menu here, but Ryan thought if there were, the name he wanted would be bright red—and maybe spelled out in flashing letters. But he said it anyway: "Take us to Herne's lair."

The mushrooms began to spin around them, first slowly, then faster. Except after a moment, Ryan realized the mushrooms weren't actually rotating; the circle of bare earth they all stood upon was spinning. Weirdly, there was no sensation of movement, and it didn't *feel* like they were on the world's fastest merry-go-round. The mushrooms and trees all around blurred in a frenzy of motion until they formed a wall of streaky green and white and red. Gabriel whistled. "Not bad, Rye. Not bad."

The whirling of their surroundings slowed, taking on a grayish cast instead of red and green, and gradually slowed to a stop. They weren't in a ring of mushrooms anymore, but in the center of a group of rectangular stones standing in a circle, each at least a dozen feet high and five or six feet across. "We're here," Ryan said. The stones were close together, with gaps only a couple of feet wide between them. Tom Dockin would have been trapped inside, probably, unless he knocked the stones over—it was for the best he hadn't come. The Trow King grunted, approached one of the gaps, tried to shoulder his way through, and sighed. He did his amoeba-like splitting trick again, and the two smaller versions of him stepped through two separate gaps, pausing to reform on the other side. "Seems safe enough," he called. "But we have another problem."

Ryan and the others twisted sideways and squeezed through the cracks between the stones, and joined the Trow King.

"Oh, no," Silas said, his voice low, almost a whimper. "No, no, no."

"Not good," Gabriel agreed. "But you have to admit, we *are* close to Herne's wood."

The standing stones took up most of the available space, because they were standing on a small, rocky island in the middle of an algae-slimed lake. Will-o-the-wisps bobbed in the distance, green and white and yellow floating balls of light. The nearest shore of the lake was only about fifty yards away . . . but the lake and the island were at the center of an enormous hedge maze that stretched off for miles in every direction. From the slight elevation of the island, Ryan could see along a few of the paths leading through the maze, but not well enough to trace a way out. The maze seemed to go on for miles, but beyond it, straight in the direction they were facing, towered a group of dead-looking trees as tall as skyscrapers—even greater than the Great Tree!—their black trunks all wound around with vines bearing thorns the size of tanker trunks. That must be Herne's wood . . . If they could only reach it.

"Okay, the maze is going to be a pain," Ryan said, "but we'll make our way through—"

Gabriel laughed. It was, no surprise, a nasty laugh. "I would be very worried about the maze if I thought there was a chance we could actually reach it. The water is a bigger problem, though."

"The water's pretty gross-looking, but we can swim across."

"The water isn't the problem," Gabriel said. "It's the stuff that lives in the water. Some of the nastiest beasties and bogies in fairyland make their home in lakes and ponds."

"Jenny Greenteeth," Silas said. "Nelly Longarms. They live only to drown."

The water began to foam and roil, and two figures broke through to the surface. One had long green hair, and arms that were even longer, reaching out over the surface of the lake almost far enough to touch them. The other had the eyes and hair of a woman but the mouth of a deep undersea fish, with enormous green interlocking fangs. "Come in," Nelly Longarms said in a voice full of echoes and dripping. "Come down to the bottom of the lake with us." Jenny Greenteeth hissed her agreement.

"We can't fight them," the Trow King said. "The water is their element. They'd just drown us, no matter how many of me there are."

"I don't have any spells to dry up a lake," Gabriel said. "I usually avoid places like this—they're the deadliest in all of fairyland."

"I could summon the hunt," Ryan said, "but then we'd be all but defenseless when it came time to fight Herne."

"I fear we must retreat," Silas said.

Jenny and Nelly approached, water eddying around their bodies, which were dead white and clad in shreds of waterlogged fabric. Nelly's arms reached, and Jenny's teeth gnashed . . . and Ryan noticed that Puck was doing his best to hide behind one of the standing stones. "Hey," he called. "Hey, *Puck!* What are you hiding from?"

The fairy winced, and Nelly Longarms lowered her long arms. "Wait," she said, in a rather more ordinary and conversational voice. "Is *Puck* up there? Puck, you old trickster! You never visit us anymore!"

"Ladies," he said, stepping into view, looking a little greenish himself. "You know how things are. I've been busy."

Nelly elbowed Jenny Greenteeth. "Ha, he's been *busy.* You hear that? Sure he has. Busy chasing after fairy princesses, I bet—"

"He speaks the truth," the Trow King rumbled. "The Horned Lord trapped him in the form of a cup."

"A *cup?*" Nelly said. "You mean, a drinking vessel?"

"I'm afraid so," Puck said. "And even now, I don't have my full, ah, complement of abilities—"

"You mean you can't become a kelpie." Nelly crossed her long arms over her chest and scowled at him. "Or a selkie. Or anything useful. Even though you *said* you'd come back and frolic with us under the surface again."

"I wish I could!" Puck said. "I think often of that *bracing* afternoon I spent with you and your dear sister Jenny. The memories are among my fondest. But, as I said, I lack my usual ability to take on new shapes, and moreover, I'm on something of . . . well, call it a quest. Do you think we could pass by? If so, I'll return at my earliest convenience." Puck's smile was as radiant as a sun. Ryan figured his charisma stats must be off the charts (In the game, if you had a high enough charisma score, you could talk your way out of situations that would normally get you killed. That probably explained how Puck had stayed alive as long as he had).

"Hmm," Nelly said. "We're supposed to drown anyone who tries to step off that island. It's one of the Horned Lord's great weaknesses, you know, having this circle of stones so close to the wood. That's why he dug this lake and grew that maze."

Jenny made a grinding, bubbling, chortling sort of noise, and Nelly nodded. "She's right. What kind of guardians would we be if we just let you go by without even trying to drown you?"

"There's still the maze," Silas said. "It looks quite fearsome."

"Totally impossible to solve," Nelly said. "Enchanted to cause confusion and delay. No chance you'd ever make it through. You mortals would starve to death walking in circles, and Puck and the Trow fellow would come crawling back to us just for a drink of water."

"If the maze is certain death anyway," Ryan said, "what's the harm in letting us pass?"

Jenny gurgled and Nelly nodded. "He does have a point. Puck, do you promise to come spend a day with us as soon as you have your abilities back?"

"Nothing would give me more pleasure, my darling—"

"Ha, I'm not overmuch concerned with your pleasure, Robin Goodfellow. I want to hear you say the words 'I promise.'"

Puck squirmed, gritted his teeth, and finally said, "If you give my friends and me safe passage, I promise to come visit you and your sister as soon as I regain my powers."

"Fair enough," Nelly said. "Jenny, let's withdraw our influence a bit, eh?" Nelly and Jenny sank back beneath the water, and the level of water in the lake fell . . . but only right in front of them. After a few moments, a strip of soggy, algae-slimed land stretched from the island to the shore. Puck stepped onto it, and the others followed tentatively, Ryan trying hard not to imagine the water slamming back down over them.

But they made it to shore safely and stepped onto solider ground, the mud of the lake bottom sucking at their shoes. Once they were all free, the water flowed back into place rather placidly, and Jenny and Nelly rose again. Jenny had half a fish speared on her forest of needle-sharp teeth, and she devoted most of her attention to eating it. Nelly called, "Watch out for the thorns. They're poisonous. And the hedges move. Otherwise there's nothing much to worry about. You'll just die of boredom, unless you starve first—No, wait. I tell a lie. It's thirst that kills you mortals fastest, isn't it? I wouldn't know. I've never had anyone in my company die of *thirst*. There's plenty of water around whenever I see someone die. Usually they're swallowing it by the gallon." On that cheerful note, Nelly waved with one of her long arms and sank under the water. Jenny swallowed the last of her fish, gave a jaunty wave of her own, and dove down as well.

"Sweet girls," the Trow King said. "Why did you try to hide from them, Puck?"

"We parted on uncomfortable terms, last time I visited them. Ryan, Silas, Gabriel," Puck said, "let me give you a piece of advice: Never, ever, ever attempt to date a pair of sisters at the same time. If I teach you nothing else, let me teach you that."

"Um, okay." Ryan surveyed the path before them: a gravel track, just wide enough for two to walk side by side, leading into a hedge maze where the hedges were composed mostly of twining black briars. Every thorn had a tiny dot of transparent fluid at the end—they literally dripped poison.

"I wonder why Herne did not simply grow an impenetrable wall of thorns," Silas said. "Why offer a path at all?"

"No harm in offering a path if there's no way to navigate it," Gabriel said. "And it sows the false hope that you might eventually make it through."

"Yes," Puck agreed. "It's far crueler to make it a maze, rather than a wall. If you see a wall, you might just give up. But if you look at a maze, you feel the temptation to try and solve it."

"We will solve it," Ryan said. "These kinds of things always have a solution."

Several will-o-the-wisps drifted over and began bobbing over their heads, and then disappearing into the maze. "We know not to follow *those*," Gabriel said. "They exist solely to lead travelers astray."

Silas hmm'ed. "I wonder, then, if we only follow paths the will-o-the-wisps do *not* go down, if we might find our way through?"

"That almost makes sense," Gabriel said. "Of course, if Herne is truly ingenious, he'll expect us to think that, and send some of the will-o'-the-wisps the *right* way, knowing we won't follow."

"We could split up," the Trow King said. "I myself could split up many times."

"No, if the hedges move, we could be separated forever," Puck said. "Much better if we stay together—"

Ryan fished in his pocket and pulled out the tin whistle he'd taken from Puck's cupboard. He wasn't sure it would do anything . . . but in the game, whistles could be used to summon magical animals to fight for you or to let you ride them—or, sometimes, to guide you. He put the whistle to his lips and blew a long, silent note.

Which wasn't to say the whistle didn't make a sound—although, strictly speaking, it didn't. Instead, the whistle blew a note of utter silence. Though his friends were all still talking, their words were no longer audible. The sound of the rippling lake ceased, as did the very faint whisper of the gentle wind through the briar maze, and the sound of Ryan's own breathing—and even the sound of blood rushing in his ears, which he'd never been aware of hearing before it stopped. He ceased blowing, and sound returned, but his friends (and Gabriel) all stared at him. "What is *that*?" Gabriel said. "It would be tremendous as a weapon against vocal spell-casters—tootle it as soon as they start an incantation, then hit them over the head with a brick."

"I . . . I was just hoping it would call something, like a great silver stag or—" His voice stopped, and it didn't take magic to dry up his words. He raised his hand and pointed, and everyone turned to look along the path into the maze.

Where a very aged black Labrador retriever was limping toward them. "That's Gertie," Ryan said. "Gert. My family dog." He looked at the whistle. "This . . . It must have called her, somehow."

"How would a whistle that makes no sound—that in fact destroys sound—call any kind of dog?" Gabriel demanded.

Ryan knelt to ruffle Gert's fur, and as far as he could tell, it was really her: same old Gert smell, same old Gert fur, same sloppy tongue lap on his cheek when he got within slobbering range. "Well, she is deaf," he said. "In a way, all she can hear is silence. Old girl, I didn't mean to call you. I never expected—"

"Her name is Gert?" Silas said. "Like the Gurt Dog?"

"I don't know what that is," Ryan said, scratching behind Gert's ears.

"There are many supernatural dogs," Puck said. "Most of them are portents of doom and destruction, heralding death. The Barghest, the yeth hound, the Shug Monkey, the Cu Sith, many more that are nameless. But some few are more benevolent, like Black Shuck . . . and the Gurt Dog, or Great Dog. The Gurt Dog is said to appear to lost or solitary travelers, and to act as a protector . . . and a guide."

"I have heard those stories," Silas said.

Gert woofed softly and pushed her nose into Ryan's cheek. Then she turned and began trotting into the maze.

"Could be a trick," Gabriel Ratchet said. "One of Herne's hounds trying to lead us astray, or a shapeshifter, or—"

"That's my Gert," Ryan said. "She'll show us the way." When Ryan was younger—and, more importantly, when Gert was younger—she used to walk with him down the dirt road in front of their house the quarter mile to the bus stop every morning before school. She would invariably be waiting for him there when he came home. She'd stopped doing that a couple of years before, because she couldn't get around well anymore, but deep down he knew that she could be counted on and that her loyalty to him was absolute.

No evil hound of Herne's would lick his face in exactly that way. He followed after her, keeping to the center of the path between the thorny hedges, and she walked along, not too fast, never glancing back to see if he was following her—no more than Ryan had ever needed to look back to check that *she* was following *him* all those mornings he'd walked to catch the bus. And he knew his companions were following him too. They took many turnings through the maze, and gradually the black thorns became less numerous, and the hedges became more green, and flowers started to appear, and the paths grew wider. Gert led them, choosing turns without hesitation, nose low to the ground, but she seemed to have a harder and harder time as they trekked on, limping and lowering her head and slowing down . . . until finally she dropped in the middle of the track and closed her eyes.

"Gertie, no!" Ryan dropped to his knees beside her and stroked her fur. Gert's breathing grew ragged and slow, and tears sprang up in the corner of Ryan's eyes. She couldn't die. He'd had pet hamsters die and goldfish, and that was bad enough, but Gert was family. She'd been around as long as *he* had, and if she died now, because he'd called her away from the warmth of the house with his whistle, brought her into the Deep Woods, he'd never forgive himself. "Please, Gert, get up, okay?"

She licked his hand weakly but didn't open her eyes.

Gabriel Ratchet sighed. "I can't believe I'm about to do this," he said.

13

GABRIEL KNELT BESIDE GERT. "DUMB ANIMAL."

"Don't you hurt her," Ryan said, thinking of Gabriel's dozen cats and the terrible things he wanted to do to them. "I'll kill you if you hurt her."

"You'll have help," Puck said. "The dog has taken us from the poisonous heart of the maze—if she is going to pass away, she deserves to do so with dignity and peace, not abused by you."

"There's no point in being cruel to a *dog*," Gabriel said. "They're just stupid beasts. I like messing with creatures who understand they're being messed with—that's why I was never cruel to Tom Dockin. He's too doglike. Oh, I took advantage of him, but I didn't torment him any more than I would this animal. What you all must think of me. I'm going to do something extraordinarily kind instead. Much as it pains me." Gabriel rested one hand on the back of Gert's neck, and reached out with his other hand to grasp one of the flowering branches bobbing down from the wall of the hedge maze. He closed his eyes and gritted his teeth and made a strange hissing sound, as if trying to whistle without using his lips. The flower on the branch he was grasping turned black and dropped its petals, and the leaves turned brown. The branch, once supple and green, twisted and dried up, and the life-sapping power of Gabriel's spell traveled up the branch to the hedge. Soon fifty more flowers dropped their petals, and hundreds more leaves withered, creating an ugly patch on the hedge the size of a garage door.

Gert, meanwhile, stopped breathing so heavily, and stood up, and began to wag her tail, and woofed happily. Ryan couldn't be sure, but he thought there was less gray in her muzzle now too.

"You have healing magic?" Silas said. "*You?*"

"Life-stealing magic," Gabriel corrected, scowling. "Though, yes, the life stolen can be redirected. I learned it to heal myself, but it works just as well on lesser beings."

Ryan grinned, patted Gert, and laughed out loud. "Every adventuring party needs a healer. I didn't expect it to be *you*, Gabriel, but thank you for saving my—"

"Oh, shut up, and tell the mutt to lead us out of here."

"Do you know the way, girl?" Ryan said. Gert barked and hurried along, much faster than before, leading them around two more corners and out of the hedge maze.

"Of all the luck." Gabriel kicked at the dirt. "If I'd known we were that close to getting out, I would have left the dog where she was."

"This is it, then." Ryan stared at the landscape before them. The hedge maze opened onto a vast lawn of green grass, scattered with bits of sporting equipment: lawn darts, a sagging volleyball net, field hockey sticks, croquet mallets, pins, and balls for lawn bowling.

"This used to be the Great Lawn," Puck said. "Before Herne took over, we used to play games here on the endless summer afternoons. But Herne only loves hunting, and so he forbid us to play all other sports." He put his hand on Silas's shoulder. "I know it must be hard for you to believe, but our fairyland was not always such a hard and cruel place, Silas. Once it was a land of endless frolic, where we wanted for nothing, and where anything we desired could be had with nothing but a thought. The Horned Lord changed all that."

"If we defeat him," Silas said, "would this become a land of pleasure again?"

"We can but hope," Puck said.

Beyond the lawn rose the mighty trees of Herne's wood, bigger even than the Great Tree . . . but now that they were closer, Ryan could tell the trees were petrified: living trees turned into dead stone. The only things living in that forest were the vines of poisonous thorns winding around the trees . . . and the Horned Lord himself, brooding at the center of the dead grove.

"Do we have a plan?" Gabriel said. "Or do we just stroll in to certain death? Or, for those immortals among us, eternal torment? What can we expect when we get in there?"

"I don't know anyone who's entered Herne's wood and come back out to tell the tale," the Trow King said.

"It's said he sits on a throne of thorns, and plots, and plans, and muses," Puck said. "Beyond that, I know nothing."

Ryan spoke, reluctantly. "I, ah . . . heard some stuff. From somebody who knows. When we step inside, one of us might . . . lose control. Herne can do that—make one of us fight for him, against our will. We have to stop whoever he takes over, tie them up, get them out of the way. Then he'll unleash his hounds—we'll try to stop him with the whistle. Then, ah . . . there might be ghosts."

"Oh, good," Gabriel said. "I love ghosts."

"After that . . . we just beat up Herne. Try to knock his helmet off, is the main thing. We've got Gabriel's magic, and the Trow King's strength, and Puck's wit, and Gert's loyalty, and I have the horn—"

"But what part do I have to play?" Silas said. "I have no weapons, no magic, no great strength, no powerful artifacts—"

"You're the whole reason we're here," Ryan said. "You've been trapped in this place a hundred years, and you're still trying to break free. You've never given up, and you've faced some of your greatest fears, from Tom Dockin to Nelly Longarms, to try and escape. You're the bravest kid I've ever met, Silas. We need you to *lead* us."

"I am honored by your words, Ryan."

"And I'm nauseated," Gabriel said. "Let's get this over with."

Silas took the lead, guiding them over the wide lawn, and they soon fell into the shadow of the towering petrified trees with bark the color of wet concrete. "This is a grim place," the Trow King said. "And my people live underneath a large flat rock in a hole full of snakes, so I know about grim."

The massive trees disappeared into the clouds, and up close they seemed like doorless, windowless buildings, all built far too close together. Silas didn't hesitate but led them between two of the vine-twisted pillars and into the dark between. The "streets" among the trees were narrow and diverged quickly, with half a dozen branching paths in different directions. "Another maze," Gabriel said. "Does the dog have any advice?"

Gert whimpered, her tail lowered, and stayed close to Ryan.

"We may choose any path," Silas said. "All will lead eventually to the center of the grove, and to Herne. Though we should be careful, in case Ryan is right, and one of us is destined to turn on the others."

"Ah," Puck said. "About that." Ryan looked back at him, and the fairy was sweating profusely, and trembling. "I feel a geas being laid upon me. A compulsion. Herne is, ah, taking over my mind . . . and worse, my body . . . "

"Give me the poker," Gabriel said, holding out his hand. "I'll just club the useless fool over the head. At least Herne didn't force one of us with actual *abilities* to be his slave."

"I'm afraid Herne has released me from those bonds as well," Puck said, and began transforming into an enormous golden-scaled snake. "I'd be delighted, under other circumstances, to have my full range of shapechanging powers back. Though I suppose when I'm done with you, Herne will make me slither over to him, so he can lay hands on me and steal my powers again." Puck's voice was no different in snake form than it had been in fairy form— or, for that matter, in cup form. The snake's eyes were black, its fangs white and its mouth opened wide as a cave. The body was longer than a school bus, and it slithered around the companions, ringing them in with its scaly body. "I'm supposed to squeeze you to death and eat the ones who won't die," Puck said. "Terribly sorry. I wish it could be otherwise. And really, a giant *snake*? Where's the humor in that? The Horned Lord could have at least allowed me—"

"Wait!" Silas shouted, as Puck lowered his serpentine head and opened his vast jaws. "You are an oathbreaker, Robin Goodfellow!"

The snake drew back. "What?"

"You made a promise to the sisters of the lake," Silas said, standing directly beneath the great snake's snout. "Do you remember?"

"Ah, I promised to return to them as soon as I regained the power to shapeshift. But I can't! Herne has laid a geas on me, extracting an oath of obedience against my will and forcing me to do his bidding—"

"Fairy law," Gabriel Ratchet said smugly. "Don't you know anything?" As if he hadn't lost his giant servant just hours ago because of his own ignorance of fairy law. "When obeying one order means breaking another, the earlier promise wins."

Puck uncoiled and sank back into a relatively human-looking form. "Why, you're right! Herne's compulsion has no power if it forces me to break another promise!" He smiled, dazzlingly bright, but then his face fell. "Of course, that means I have to return to Nelly and Jenny and their . . . " he shuddered. "Damp and slimy hospitality. So my ability to change shape won't be any help in your battle against the Horned Lord."

"Go," Silas said. "Keep your promise. *Not* eating us is help enough."

"Good luck, bold friends," Puck said, bowing. "I hope to see you all emerge from the trees soon." He took a few steps and then turned into a red-winged bird and flew away.

"You predicted the betrayal all right," Gabriel said to Ryan. "So what's next?"

"Herne sets his hounds on us," Ryan said.

"Oh, is *that* all."

"Let us face him, then." Silas rested the iron poker on his shoulder and walked along the path. When the thorns grew too close, he set about him with the iron tool, bashing the vines away and clearing the way. When they proved too numerous for him to hack through, Gabriel muttered a spell and made the vines blacken and shrivel as if they'd been burned, but without smoke or fire. "I think he's afraid of us," the Trow King said. "Why else try to keep us away with thorns?"

"He expected Puck to trouble us more than he did," Silas said. "He underestimated us."

Yes! Ryan thought. *Silas is starting to believe we can win this!*

With a last strike to knock down a thick lattice of vines and thorns, Silas cleared the way to the center of the grove. A great chair, which appeared to have grown from vines and briars rather than being built, dominated the center of the room, and Herne the Horned Lord sat there, lit by four flickering torches on tall poles. Herne wore the heavy armor from the game, his sharpened antlers glittering in the torchlight. "Children," he called, his voice booming like a wooden spoon banging on the bottom of a metal pot. "I will give you one last chance to turn back, and then I will summon my hunt . . . and they will make you their prey."

"No, we will give *you* one final chance," Silas said. "Free me, and free Gabriel, and swear an oath to steal no more human children, and we will let you continue to rule this place."

"So be it." The Horned Lord lifted a ram's horn in one gauntleted hand. His horn was easily twice the size of Ryan's, and he put the mouthpiece up to the mouth hole in his helmet.

Ryan started blowing the tin whistle, and waves of silence filled the grove—Gert was clearly howling, though you couldn't hear it—but the sound of Herne's horn cut through clearly, all the more impressive because it was the only sound in the world. A low, deep, bone-vibrating tone, far more powerful than any horn call Ryan had ever heard through the speakers of his computer, and far louder than it had been the last time Herne had blown the horn, outside Gentle Annie's cave.

Ryan dropped the useless tin whistle, and Herne laughed. "Did you think a little toy like that could stop the sound of my best horn? Boy, even the *dead* can hear that call."

Barking and baying and howling filled the air, along with the strange sound of dozens of animal feet running along the forest floor. Gert lowered her head and growled menacingly, but what hope did she have of fighting off the Wild Hunt? Ryan considered blowing his own horn . . . but would that let him take over Herne's hunt, or just summon a *separate* hunt, which would attack Herne's? Being stuck in the middle of a vast supernatural dogfight seemed like a bad idea, but what other choice did he have?

"I've got this," the Trow King said, and began to divide into multiple, smaller versions of himself.

The hounds appeared from the pathways behind the thorn throne. Some were headless, but howled all the same. Some were the black of spilled motor oil, complete with the shimmer of rainbows deep in their coats. Some were the size of small cars, and others were the size of ordinary dogs, but glowing like fireflies. A few had huge eyes, big as saucers and perfectly white. One had three heads on one body. Among the hounds there were small men—elves, Ryan thought—carrying bows and arrows and taking aim.

"Run, children!" Herne shouted. "Run, and give my hunt some exercise!"

Instead, the Trow King—by now there were dozens of him, most no larger than small housecats—launched themselves at the hounds, screaming a joyous battle cry from countless throats. The smaller the Trow King got, the stronger he got, but even knowing that, Ryan was astonished to see the Trow Kings pick up the first hounds to arrive and hurl them at their fellows in the next rank. Soon the Trow Kings were knocking over elves, stealing their weapons, climbing onto the backs of hounds, and whipping the dogs onward by hitting them in the flanks with broken arrow shafts. Some of the Trow Kings were even riding on the shoulders of the elves, just like Gabriel used to ride on Tom Dockin, and the elves didn't look too happy about it. The pack reached Silas, Gabriel, and Ryan, but by then all of them were bearing little Trow Kings, and none stopped to attack, as the Trow King urged them past, out of the throne room. After a few moments, nothing was left of the Wild Hunt but churned-up dirt from hundreds of feet, a few broken arrows, and the already-fading sound of distant baying.

"Hmm," Herne said. "Fine. I'll let your own past violence be the end of you, then." And he blew his horn a second time, a lower, more melancholy note that made Ryan's teeth hurt.

"The ghosts," he said. "This is when he summons the ghosts of everything we've ever killed."

"I've never killed anything," Silas said.

"Me neither," Ryan said. They both looked at Gabriel.

"What? You're saying our impending doom is *my* fault? I never thought I'd have to face the consequences of my actions!"

But no ghosts attacked them. Herne twisted around on his throne and looked behind him, growling low in his throat.

"Are those . . . flies?" Silas said, waving his hand at the air. Tiny houseflies, white instead of black, buzzed around their heads. A line of white ants—not the white of termites, but ants the actual color of snow or milk—trundled into the throne room, and a few ghostly spiders scuttled in.

"Ha," Ryan said. "I *have* killed some flies and stepped on some ants in my life. Sorry, little guys." He glanced at Gabriel. "I guess you're not as dangerous as you like to make out."

"I live in fairyland," Gabriel muttered. "Almost everything here is immortal. It's not my fault if immortals won't die. It's a good thing he didn't summon the spirits of everyone we'd seriously *injured*, I'll tell you that much. We'd be dead."

"Right." None of the ghostly bugs went near Gabriel, just Ryan and Silas, which meant *they* were more deadly than Gabriel Ratchet was. And that meant . . . No, there was no time to think it through now. They still had Herne to deal with. Ryan turned to the Horned Lord. "So that's it, huh? Now we just fight you."

"I can't believe you're making me get up from my chair," he said, standing and loosening a dagger at his belt. "If you've never killed anything other than bugs, what makes you think you can defeat me?"

"This," Ryan said, and blew Herne's second-best horn. The tone wasn't quite as bone shaking as the one from Herne's own horn . . . but it wasn't bad and it worked.

The hounds returned—still bearing the little Trow Kings on their backs. But this time, they came from behind Ryan and raced for the Horned Lord.

Herne took a step backward. "No! I am your master! I forbid this!"

"You should run, Herne," Gabriel said.

"I. Do not. RUN! Herne is not *prey*."

"We'll see," Silas said quietly, and then the hounds were upon him.

Herne stood his ground, slashing about with his dagger, but within moments the hounds and huntsman had knocked him off his feet. Even Gert dove in, joining the fray. The Horned Lord tried to stand, but the Hunt drove him down again, teeth snapping at his armor and elves tearing the metal away, until Herne was entirely unarmored—except for his helmet and its towering antlers.

"Enough!" Ryan shouted, and the hounds all turned to look at him. The Trow King, who'd already dismounted and reassembled himself into a single body, stopped trying to wrench off Herne's helmet and stepped back. The hounds raced away, their elvish hunters running with them, and soon the throne room was silent again.

Silas and Ryan walked to the Horned Lord. Herne was kneeling, head lowered, pale and wiry body scratched and bleeding. Silas lifted the poker high and brought it down on one of Herne's metal antlers. The crash of impact was deafening, like a close-up car crash, but the sharpened antler snapped off at the base and fell into the dirt. Silas handed the poker to Ryan, who struck off the other antler with a heavy blow—the jolt of contact made his whole arm hurt up to the shoulder, and the other antler snapped off.

Silas lifted the helmet off Herne's head and threw it into the dirt, revealing the face of a bearded, thin, tired-looking man. "I am defeated," Herne said. "My rule depended on never being bested, and you have bested me. All oaths and bonds to me are broken. You are free."

Ryan touched the poker to Herne's chest, over the heart. "Not good enough," he said. "Tell Silas who you really are."

"Ooh, yes, true confession time," Gabriel said, joining them.

"All right," Herne said. "The truth. I was once a human, like you, and I came to this place—"

"No, *Boneless*," Ryan said. "Not the *fake* truth. The actual truth. About what you are. What this place is."

"What do you mean?" Silas stared at him, frowning, and Ryan felt bad—making his friend frown in what should have been his moment of triumph—but if they were *really* going to win, Silas had to know what they were fighting for . . . and against.

"Yes," Herne said. "What do you mean? I was once a human hunter, but—"

"You're a *fake*," Ryan said. "There's no Herne the hunter, not really. Just come clean! Silas, you have to understand, none of this is *real*. It's all just, like, a nightmare you're having while you're awake—"

"You seem tired, my friend," Silas said, his face more solemn than ever. "We have been through great travails this day. I am afraid the strain has been too much for you. Perhaps you should rest?"

The shadows all around them grew darker, and Herne lifted his head, a hideous grin on his face, but Silas didn't notice. Herne picked up one of his snapped-off antlers and held it, jagged end gleaming, like a knife.

Crap, it's all slipping away from me, Ryan thought desperately. *If I can't convince Silas about the Boneless, we'll fail again. We'll* both *be trapped here. The Boneless will win.* If he only had a magic sword instead of a stupid fireplace poker maybe he could . . .

Ryan closed his eyes and gritted his teeth. Of course he had a magic sword. He was here at the final boss battle in *Wild Hunt Online*. You couldn't come this far *without* getting a magical sword. In the game, they were common as dirt. Sometimes you'd kill a dire sheep or a walking tree or something and find a magic sword stuck in its fur or branches. You'd have to make an effort *not* to get a magic sword . . .

The iron poker shifted in his hand, grew heavier and longer, but strength seemed to flow into his arms from the handle, and he opened his eyes.

Silas gasped. "Ryan. What is that?"

"I changed the world," Ryan said, holding up the sword. The weapon wasn't any longer than the poker had been—it was a short sword, Ryan supposed—with a handle made of wood carved in a leaf-and-branches design, and a rectangular iron handguard, and a long, gleaming blade. Deep blue-and-green lights—signs of magic—twinkled up and down the blade like fireflies. "That's what I'm trying to tell you, Silas—this place is only what we *make* it."

"That's the stupidest thing I've ever heard," Gabriel said, rolling his eyes. "The world is what it *is*, and you and Silas are just insects scurrying in the dirt." When Silas looked over at Gabriel, frowning, Herne readied himself to spring, the broken edge of the antler gleaming in his hand.

Ryan stepped behind Gabriel, put one arm around the bigger boy's chest, and pressed the point of his sword gently into the hollow at the base of Gabriel's throat. "Be still, everyone. Now, tell the truth, Boneless, or I'll kill Gabriel." He paused. "I'll kill your *son*."

14

"Well, crap," Gabriel said. "This was unexpected."

"What?" Silas said, taking a step back and looking at Herne, who tossed his antler away in disgust. "Gabriel . . . is the Horned Lord's son?"

"Not exactly," Ryan said. "'Son' isn't quite the right word. I don't know what the right word is. He's more like a . . . fingernail clipping? A clone? A seedling? Tell him, Boneless. Show your real self."

"It's not that easy," Herne pleaded, still kneeling in the dirt. "I have my limitations—"

"Silas," Ryan said, keeping a tight grip on Gabriel, though the "boy" wasn't struggling. "Do you remember, when you came into the woods for the first time, seeing something really disgusting?"

"I . . . Yes. A great blob of flesh, on the forest floor, growing around a tree. Like a pudding made of skin. Horrendous, shapeless, but always in motion."

"What did you think it was?"

"The Boneless," Silas said. "The It. My mother told me about it—a shapeless something that slides alongside the road, terrifying travelers. I ran away from the creature, and soon heard the fairy music, and met other creatures of fairyland, and before long was trapped here—"

"But it started with the Boneless," Ryan said. "This thing, which is pretending to be Herne. Show him your true self."

Herne sighed, and—perhaps because Silas believed what Ryan said—the Horned Lord slumped and melted into a sort of puddle of wet wax and hairless skin, a puckered mouth on top opening and closing. "Here. Here. See me. See what I am."

"This is the only real supernatural creature in the forest," Ryan said. "It's a monster that feeds on your imagination. Everything else in fairyland . . . is just things it invented, dreams or nightmares or memories or imaginings it found in your mind and brought to life."

"Can this be true?" Silas said.

"You expected fairies." Ryan shrugged. "Because of the stories your mother told you. So this thing, which we might as well call the Boneless even though it doesn't really *have* a name, showed you fairies. If you'd thought you'd died and gone to heaven, it would have shown you angels and clouds and guys with harps. If you'd believed there were savage Indians in the woods, you would have found yourself living in a Western. The Boneless doesn't care—it just uses what it finds in your mind, and brings it to life, and eats it. But I shouldn't have called it a monster. I don't think it means any harm—I'm not sure it can even think, unless we give it a mind to think with."

"All right," Silas said slowly, and the thorn throne gradually faded from sight, and the massive petrified skyscraper trees became ordinary very tall trees, and the thorn vines curled up on themselves and disappeared. The sun was fading toward the horizon, and it was nearly dusk. Now they were just three boys and an elderly dog standing in the woods—the Trow King had disappeared at some point, and Ryan hadn't even noticed—surrounding something like a waterbed made of flesh. Silas looked at Gabriel. "But you said he is this thing's son. How can it have a son?"

"Show him what you are, Gabriel," Ryan said.

"I'm Gabriel Ratchet, a boy like you, tricked by this thing just like Silas was—"

Ryan closed his eyes. He pushed the sword point deep into Gabriel's neck, as hard as he could, inches of iron sliding into the flesh. Silas gasped and Gabriel grunted. Gert had no comment.

Releasing the sword and stepping back, Ryan opened his eyes. Gabriel wasn't bleeding, despite the fact that he had a sword sticking through his neck. It looked like some sort of trick for Halloween, like a fake axe or an arrow sticking through someone's head, totally unreal. "Fine," Gabriel said, his voice harsh and grating because of the metal in his throat. He crossed his arms and scowled. "I just want to know how you figured it out."

Ryan shrugged. "People I talked to in fairyland kept forgetting about you. They'd talk about the boys in the Deep Woods, but they only mentioned Silas and me, never you. So I figured you weren't really a boy at all. Plus, my imagination affected this place—things I thought about appeared here, but nothing ever changed when you were around, and even if you *did* sell off your memories, that seemed weird. Since you went into the real world to see my parents, I thought you might be more than just an illusion—that you might be a part of the Boneless itself, sort of . . . snipped off and walking around on your own. Was I right?"

"Close enough," Gabriel muttered.

"What was the point of you, originally?" Ryan said.

"To make life so unbearable for Silas that he'd try to escape."

Silas gaped. "You *wanted* me to escape? Then why not set me free?"

"We tried, you . . . you bloody *pessimist*!" Gabriel shouted and wrenched the sword from his throat, leaving a bloodless hole. "We kept setting you free, but you always thought it was a joke or a trap or a trick, so you kept getting dragged back. You've kept us here for a bloody century, when there's a whole *world* we could be—" He broke off.

"That's the other thing you're for," Ryan said. He nodded to Silas. "We were supposed to believe Gabriel was a real boy—really believe it. Believe it enough for him to keep looking like a real boy even after we defeated Herne and set you free from fairyland. Then Gabriel, who's really just a piece of the Boneless in disguise, would get to go free too, and move out into the world, and feed on the imaginations of everyone he encountered."

"But if the Boneless can conjure whole worlds . . . " Silas said.

Ryan nodded. "Can you imagine? Everything any little kid was scared of would come to life. There really would be monsters under the bed."

"But it could be great things too!" Gabriel said. "Good imaginings! Lollipop trees and rivers of chocolate milk and dragons you could ride to school and—"

"But you're *cruel*, Gabriel," Ryan said. "So it wouldn't be all those good

119

things, would it? We can't let you out into the world, not with the things you can do—it's too dangerous."

Gabriel Ratchet smiled his terrible smile. "And how will you stop me, little boy? You can't kill me. You've already seen that."

Ryan took a step toward the boy, who wasn't a boy. "Gabriel," he said. "We don't *believe* in you anymore."

Gabriel moaned and began to melt, slumping just as Herne had, until he was a smaller puddle of wax and meat like the rest of the Boneless. His mass slithered and oozed over to the main body and flowed into it, like two globs of gravy flowing together. The sword was just a length of iron again now, resting on the forest floor.

"You and I are the only real things in this wood," Silas said. "It is hard to believe . . . but I do believe it."

"Well, Gert's real," Ryan said, scratching her behind the ears. "I wasn't sure, before, but she definitely is. And the trees are real. And, I mean . . . the *Boneless* is real. The things it showed you aren't, but there *is* magic in this wood. A creature that can make the things you imagine come true. But now we know what it is, and it can't trick us. Silas, you're *free*—really free. You can come home with me. Maybe I can convince my mom and dad to let you stay with me—"

But Silas slowly shook his head. "I cannot go, Ryan. For one thing, I do not belong in your world. It is a hundred years beyond my time. My family is gone. My friends too—except for you. And if your parents did not take me in, what would happen to me?"

Ryan opened his mouth, then closed it again. His mom and dad were okay parents, but they might not be willing to take on another son, especially one who insisted he was older than Ryan's great-grandparents. And even though Silas had survived a century in a dangerous fairyland, surviving in the real world would be a lot tougher. "Look, we'll figure it out. You can live in the clubhouse and I'll bring you food—"

"But what about this?" Silas gestured to the Boneless, which was slowly oozing its way deeper into the woods. "It has such power. To conjure worlds. To keep me young forever. How can we let it go free?"

"We could dig a hole," Ryan said doubtfully. "Or *burn it* . . . ." He sighed.

"But the Boneless is alive. No smarter than a sponge stuck to a coral reef in the ocean, but still alive. It wouldn't be right to burn it, because it's not *evil*, I don't think . . . The Boneless is sort of like fire, in a way. Fire can be awesome—the fireplace keeps my house warm in the winter, and without fire you can't *make* things—like this iron poker—or cook food, or heat water, or anything. But fire can burn down houses and destroy whole cities too. It's not good or evil. It's just a question of how it's used. Like the Boneless."

"Perhaps," Silas said, "I could put it to a better use. Or at least, a less dangerous one. I could be the keeper of the Boneless, as it has for so long been *my* keeper."

"What do you mean? How would you do that?"

"I could . . . imagine," Silas said, and the trees shimmered, becoming green and lush and alive instead of red and gold and dying. "Just because I know what the Boneless *is* does not mean I cannot imagine. The Boneless is power, like a wizard's staff, a magic amulet—but I can be the one to guide that power, and protect the world. Because I know how horrible that power can be if it is misused."

"Huh." Ryan held out his hand and thought, and a bow appeared in his grasp, dark curving wood carved all over with eyes, just like the weapon his character had in the game. "I couldn't do this before, and *I* knew about the Boneless!"

"You were fighting the strength of my vision, though," Silas said. "My . . . darker world view."

"I guess so. And you'd been here so long, imagined so much so deeply, it was a pretty serious vision."

"Boneless, come to me," Silas said. The mass paused, then flowed back in his direction. "I will continue to feed you," he said. "And you will remake fairyland . . . but one without the darkness. One where it is always summer, and no one is a slave, and there is no Horned Lord, no Gabriel Ratchet, no child-eating giants." He paused. "Jenny Greenteeth and Nelly Longarms can be there. They are not so bad."

"Will this work?" Ryan said. "I mean, trying to do it on purpose?"

"Which is the more powerful act of imagination, Ryan? A dream over which you have no control or a conscious creation—a work of art?"

"Huh. You think this place can be your work of art?"

"I do," Silas said. "I believe it *very much*." He stared at the Boneless as he said this, and the mass quivered.

"Then I don't see why it won't work," Ryan said. "You're really okay, staying here? With . . . I don't know . . . imaginary friends?"

"I'm not *imaginary*," Puck said, dropping down from a tree. "Admittedly, I'm a projection of Mr. Lumpy there on the ground, my precise shape dictated by Silas's imaginings, but I *do* have an objective reality. The Boneless will be Silas's friend . . . with many, many faces."

"And that's okay with you?" Ryan said. "You don't still want to take over the world?"

Puck shrugged. "If Silas doesn't think the Boneless is a child-stealing, tyrannical, conquering evil king with horns, then it *won't* be. You see?"

"I will keep the Boneless from troubling anyone else," Silas said. "No monsters will emerge from under the beds of children. And I . . . " He looked around. "I will get almost everything I ever dreamed of."

"Ryan!" a distant voice called. "Dinnertime!"

"Wow," Ryan said. "I, uh . . . I have to go, I guess. You're sure you won't come with me? To the real world?"

"I missed my chance to live in the real world and grow up and have a normal life," Silas said. "This is my life now, and by keeping watch over the Boneless, I can make my life mean something—which is more than I ever had before."

"Ryan!" his mom called. They weren't even that far from his yard. Crazy. He opened his hand and dropped the magical bow, and it disappeared before hitting the ground.

"Okay, well, I'll visit. I mean, all I have to do is walk into the woods, right? And here you'll be—"

"I will have to close the borders," Silas said. "Much as they were sealed before. To keep others from wandering into the dominion of the Boneless and being snared by its influence. Do you understand? I can't . . . I can't just let *anyone* in here."

"Yeah," Ryan said, scuffing at the leaf-litter on the ground with his toe. "Not just anyone. I understand." He sighed.

"You have saved my life, Ryan." Silas put his arms around his friend and gave him a long hug. "You have given me a *reason* to live. Farewell."

"Yes, farewell," Puck said.

Beag's daughters strolled in, laughing together, and waved. "Goodbye, Ryan!"

The Trow King, housecat sized, tugged at the cuff of his pants. "Bye, Rye."

"Bye, bye, bye!" cried a line of goblin men who went tramping past—or maybe it was "Buy, buy, buy!" Who could tell?

Silas released him. "Take care of yourself, my friend. And thank you. I owe you a debt I can never repay."

"Anytime," Ryan said, unwilling to step away and leave all this magic behind—but his mother was calling, louder and more frequently. "Come on, Gert," he said. "Back to the real world." He waved to Silas and the others, and stepped through a pair of tree trunks toward home, and when he looked back, the woods were empty. Gert woofed once, and he went on into the yard.

"There you are!" his mother said, standing on the porch. "I was afraid you'd walked halfway to Canada."

"Way farther than that," Ryan said and went up the steps to have dinner.

15

RYAN DID HIS BEST TO GO BACK TO HIS ORDINARY LIFE over the next week—going to school, doing chores, playing *Wild Hunt Online* alone (and with his mom and dad on game night)—but he spent every moment he could in the woods, hoping to find some fragment of magic left behind. He sat alone in the clubhouse, and climbed as high as he could in trees, and pushed through tangles of underbrush he'd never bothered to cross before. He found lots of cool things—a little pile of bleached animal bones, a rusted license plate from Alaska, chunks of unidentifiable twisted metal, a tree stump that looked like a face in profile, even a big sheet of tin he used to make a little lean-to. But nothing *magical* and no sign of Silas or the world of the Boneless at all. Which just meant his friend was doing his job right, keeping the world safe from the monsters the Boneless could conjure. But after being neck deep in magic for a day, the rest of the world seemed somehow shallow in comparison.

About a week after his adventure with Silas, Ryan was changing into his pajamas when his mom yelled from the laundry room, "Rye, why can't you empty your pockets? What if I'd put these pants in the laundry, with all these leaves and trail mix crumbs and bits of twig, and—hey, what's this coin?"

Ryan pulled his shirt on over his head and hurried to the laundry room, which was full of giant piles of laundry, as usual. His parents only managed to do laundry once every couple of weeks. "Coin? What coin?" His mom was holding up a pair of his pants—the ones he'd worn to Fairyland.

"Huh, how about that," she said, looking at something in her hand. "Did you find this in the woods?" She put a dark, small coin on top of the dryer. It showed the head of an Indian chief with a feathered headdress, and the words "United States of America" running around the outside, and the date "1898" at the bottom. "It's an Indian Head penny," she said. "Haven't seen one of those in ages. I don't think they're worth much, especially as beat up as this one is, but it's pretty neat."

"Yeah, I found it in the woods," he said, picking it up. Eighteen ninety-eight . . . Silas must have slipped it into his pocket, maybe when they hugged goodbye. And that meant . . . "I'm going to put in my room."

His mom patted his shoulder. "Good idea. You'll really treasure that someday."

I treasure it now, he thought.

Alone in his room, he opened his hand and looked at the coin again.

It had changed. The Indian Head penny was just a glamour—or else, *this* was the glamour and the coin was really one Silas had kept in his pocket for more than a hundred years. Who cared? Now it was bigger, and shiny golden, and on one side it had a picture of a tree. On the other side, it had a picture of a door.

Ryan grinned and squeezed the coin tight in his fist.

Late that night, while his parents were sleeping, Ryan slipped on his shoes and crept out of the house. Gert followed him but kept silent, so he didn't mind. The yard was pitch dark, but he knew his way perfectly, so he walked toward the deeper darkness of the trees. The coin in his hand seemed to get warmer as he entered the forest . . .

And then he was in the Deep Woods. Glowing will-o-the-wisps floated around, and a crowd of fairies laughed and drank from huge cups around a bonfire. Silas and Puck rose from the log where they were sitting and waved to him. "You came!" Silas said. "Took you long enough."

"You tricked me!" Ryan said. "You made me think you were closing fairy-land to me too!"

Silas smiled—grinned, really. "You won the battle as much as I did, Ryan. More so. You have the right to come and go as you please. I was beginning to worry you might never find the coin, though—I thought I would have to leave another one in the clubhouse. Still, you must admit, it was a good joke."

"Ho! Ho! Ho!" Puck shouted.

"I shouldn't stay long," Ryan said. "I've got to go to church in the morning, so I should get some sleep, and anyway, if Mom or Dad notice I'm gone, they'll go crazy."

"Ah," Silas said, putting his arm around his friend's shoulders. "But this is fairyland. Time is different here. While you visit me, Ryan, you will not grow any older, and when you step out of the trees, it will be only moments later than the time you entered. The Boneless can do these things for us."

"A place where time stands still? That's awesome! I could find all sorts of uses for that." Ryan accepted a cup filled with what smelled like fresh apple cider. "Especially when I wait until the last minute to study for a test or do a project at school—I can come here in the morning and do it before I even catch the bus!"

"I suppose. But I was thinking more that you could do things like, oh . . . leave Gert here, so she would grow no older and would never have to die."

"Wow." He petted Gert, and she wagged her tail—Gabriel's healing spell had seemed to fade before, but now that she was back in the Deep Woods, she was acting like a puppy again. "Oh, wow." He took a sip of the cider—better even than he'd imagined—and then said, "Whoa! Silas, if I could get a wireless signal back here . . . I could play *Wild Hunt Online* as much as I *want*! I could teach you to play!"

"You see?" Silas's smile was brighter than the bonfire. "The possibilities are endless."

The End

Acknowledgments

THANKS FIRST TO MY SON RIVER, WHO MADE ME WANT TO write a book about boys on an adventure. (He adores both playing in the woods and playing video games, making him more like Ryan than I ever expected he would be when I started this story.) Thanks to my wife Heather Shaw for her unfailing support. Finally, many thanks to the whole PS Publishing team, particularly Pete and Nicky Crowther, and Nick Gevers. I've dreamed of publishing a book with them for over a decade now, and isn't it lovely when dreams come true?